OXFORD BOOKWORMS LIBRARY
Classics

Barchester Towers

Stage 6 (2500 headwords)

Series Editor: Jennifer Bassett
Founder Editor: Tricia Hedge
Activities Editors: Jennifer Bassett and Christine Lindop

ANTHONY TROLLOPE

Barchester Towers

Retold by
Clare West

OXFORD UNIVERSITY PRESS

OXFORD
UNIVERSITY PRESS

Great Clarendon Street, Oxford OX2 6DP

Oxford University Press is a department of the University of Oxford.
It furthers the University's objective of excellence in research, scholarship,
and education by publishing worldwide in

Oxford New York

Auckland Cape Town Dar es Salaam Hong Kong Karachi
Kuala Lumpur Madrid Melbourne Mexico City Nairobi
New Delhi Shanghai Taipei Toronto

With offices in

Argentina Austria Brazil Chile Czech Republic France Greece
Guatemala Hungary Italy Japan Poland Portugal Singapore
South Korea Switzerland Thailand Turkey Ukraine Vietnam

OXFORD and OXFORD ENGLISH are registered trade marks of
Oxford University Press in the UK and in certain other countries

This simplified edition © Oxford University Press 2008
Database right Oxford University Press (maker)
First published in Oxford Bookworms 2006

2 4 6 8 10 9 7 5 3

No unauthorized photocopying

All rights reserved. No part of this publication may be reproduced,
stored in a retrieval system, or transmitted, in any form or by any means,
without the prior permission in writing of Oxford University Press,
or as expressly permitted by law, or under terms agreed with the appropriate
reprographics rights organization. Enquiries concerning reproduction
outside the scope of the above should be sent to the ELT Rights Department,
Oxford University Press, at the address above

You must not circulate this book in any other binding or cover
and you must impose this same condition on any acquirer

Any websites referred to in this publication are in the public domain and
their addresses are provided by Oxford University Press for information only.
Oxford University Press disclaims any responsibility for the content

ISBN: 978 0 19 479254 7

Printed in Hong Kong

ACKNOWLEDGEMENTS

Photographs are from the BBC TV production *The Barchester Chronicles* and are
reproduced by courtesy of BBC. They feature Alan Rickman, Geraldine McEwan,
Clive Swift, Janet Maw, Susan Hampshire, and Peter Blythe

Word count (main text): 29,520 words

For more information on the Oxford Bookworms Library,
visit www.oup.com/bookworms

CONTENTS

	STORY INTRODUCTION	i
	PEOPLE IN THIS STORY	viii
	PART ONE: WAR IN BARCHESTER	
1	The new bishop	1
2	Battle begins	10
3	A rich widow	21
	PART TWO: COUNTER-ATTACK	
4	A newcomer to Barchester	32
5	Mr Slope on the attack	41
6	Two men in love	51
7	Victory for Mrs Proudie	60
	PART THREE: PEACE RETURNS	
8	The garden party	69
9	A declaration of love	78
10	A woman's friendship	86
11	The new dean	96
	GLOSSARY	106
	ACTIVITIES: Before Reading	109
	ACTIVITIES: While Reading	110
	ACTIVITIES: After Reading	113
	ABOUT THE AUTHOR	117
	ABOUT THE BOOKWORMS LIBRARY	118

PEOPLE IN THIS STORY

IN BARCHESTER
  Dr Proudie, *Bishop of Barchester*
  Mrs Proudie, *the bishop's wife*
  Olivia Proudie, *the bishop's eldest daughter*
  Mr Obadiah Slope, *the bishop's chaplain*
  Dr Trefoil, *Dean of Barchester*
  Mr Septimus Harding, *once warden of Hiram's Hospital*
  Eleanor Bold, *Mr Harding's younger daughter and a widow*
  Johnny Bold, *Eleanor's baby son*
  Mary Bold, *Eleanor's sister-in-law*
  Dr Vesey Stanhope, *a clergyman*
  Bertie Stanhope, *Dr Stanhope's son*
  Charlotte Stanhope, *Dr Stanhope's elder daughter*
  Madeline Stanhope, *also called Signora Neroni, Dr Stanhope's younger daughter*

AT PLUMSTEAD
  Dr Grantly, *the archdeacon*
  Susan Grantly, *Mr Harding's elder daughter and the archdeacon's wife*
  Mr Francis Arabin, *an Oxford clergyman*

AT PUDDINGDALE
  Mr Quiverful, *a poor country vicar*
  Mrs Quiverful, *his wife*

AT ULLATHORNE
  Mr Thorne, *the squire of Ullathorne*
  Miss Thorne, *the squire's sister*
  Lady de Courcy, *a titled neighbour of the Thornes*

BARCHESTER TOWERS

In the great cathedral cities of England, the church and politics go hand in hand. The government appoints the bishop, who is the head of the church in that city, and below him come archdeacons, deans, vicars, parsons, chaplains – all kinds of clergymen, of differing degrees of rank, importance, influence, and income.

All this is complicated enough, but the appointment of Dr Proudie as the new Bishop of Barchester overturns the old established order in that peaceful city, and a struggle for power begins against the new bishop's wife, the fearsome Mrs Proudie. And when you also add to the mixture the new bishop's chaplain, the oily and ambitious Obadiah Slope, you have a recipe for war.

And as well as the struggle for power in the church, there is also the game of love, which is played by very different rules, according to the player. Mrs Eleanor Bold, a pretty young widow, believes in honest and truthful ways of dealing with people, but she does not always understand the deceitful ways of men. The Signora Madeline Neroni, on the other hand, understands men only too well, and her beauty and her wit and her charm draw men to her, like flies into a spider's web . . .

PART ONE: WAR IN BARCHESTER

The new bishop

During the last ten days of July in the year 1852, in the ancient cathedral city of Barchester, a most important question was asked every hour and answered every hour in different ways – 'Who is to be the new bishop?'

Old Dr Grantly, who had for many years occupied the bishop's chair, was dying, just as the government of the country was about to change. The bishop's son, Archdeacon Grantly, had recently taken on many of his father's duties, and it was fairly well understood that the present prime minister would choose him as the new bishop. It was a difficult time for the archdeacon. The prime minister had never promised him the post in so many words, but those who know anything of government will be well aware that encouragement is often given by a whisper from a great man or one of his friends. The archdeacon had heard such a whisper, and allowed himself to hope.

A month ago, the doctors had said the old man would live just four more weeks. Only yesterday they had examined him again, expressed their surprise, and given him another two weeks. Now the son was sitting by his father's bedside, calculating his chances. The government would fall within five days, that much was certain; his father would die within – no, he refused to think that. He tried to keep his mind on other matters, but the race was so very close, and the prize so very great. He looked at the dying man's calm face. As far as he and the doctors could judge, life might yet hang there for weeks to come. The old bishop slept for twenty of the twenty-four hours, but during his waking moments he was able to recognize both his son and his dear old friend, Mr Harding, the archdeacon's father-in-law. Now he lay sleeping like a baby. Nothing could be easier than the old man's passing from this world to the next.

But by no means easy were the emotions of the man who sat there watching. He knew it must be now or never. He was already over fifty, and there was little chance that the next prime minister would think as kindly of him as the present one did. He thought long and sadly, in deep silence, and then at last dared to ask himself whether he really desired his father's death.

The question was answered in a moment. The proud man sank on his knees by the bedside, and, taking the bishop's hand in his own, prayed eagerly that his sins would be forgiven.

Just then the door opened and Mr Harding entered. Dr Grantly rose quickly, and as he did so, Mr Harding took both his hands and pressed them warmly. There was a stronger feeling between them than there had ever been before.

'God bless you, my dears,' said the bishop in a weak voice as he woke. 'God bless you!' and so he died.

At first neither the archdeacon nor his father-in-law knew that life was gone, but after a little while Mr Harding said gently, 'I believe it's all over. Our dear bishop is no more – dear, good, excellent old man! Well, it's a great relief, archdeacon. May all our last moments be as peaceful as his!'

In his mind Dr Grantly was already travelling from the darkened room of death to the prime minister's study. He had brought himself to pray for his father's life, but now that life was over, every minute counted. However, he did not want to

The new bishop

appear unfeeling, so he allowed Mr Harding to lead him downstairs to the sitting room. Then, when a few more moments had passed, he said, 'We should arrange for a telegraph message to be sent to the prime minister immediately.'

'Do you think it necessary?' asked Mr Harding, a little surprised. He did not know how high the archdeacon's hopes of being appointed bishop were.

'I do,' replied Dr Grantly. 'Anything might happen if we delay. Will *you* send it?'

'I? Oh, certainly. Only I don't know exactly what to say.'

Dr Grantly sat down and wrote out this message:

'By electric telegraph, for the Prime Minister at 10 Downing Street, London. The Bishop of Barchester is dead. Message sent by Mr Septimus Harding.'

'There,' he said, 'just take it to the telegraph office. Here's the money,' and he pulled a coin out of his pocket.

Mr Harding felt very much like a messenger, but he accepted the piece of paper and the coin. 'But you've put my name at the bottom, archdeacon,' he said.

Dr Grantly hesitated. How could he sign such a note himself? 'Well, yes,' he said, 'there should be the name of some clergyman, and who more suitable than an old friend like yourself? But I beg you, my dear Mr Harding, not to lose any time.'

Mr Harding got as far as the door of the room, when he suddenly remembered the news which he had come to tell his son-in-law, and which the bishop's death had driven from his mind. 'But archdeacon,' he said, turning back, 'I forgot to tell you – the government has fallen!'

'Fallen!' repeated the archdeacon, in a voice which clearly expressed his anxiety. After a moment's thought he said, 'We had better send the message anyway. Do it at once, my dear friend – a few minutes' time is of the greatest importance.'

Mr Harding went out and sent the message. Within thirty minutes of leaving Barchester, it arrived on the prime minister's desk in London. The great man read it, then sent it on to the man who was to take his place. In this way our unfortunate friend the archdeacon lost his chance of becoming a bishop.

There was much discussion in the newspapers about who would take old Dr Grantly's place. *The Jupiter*, that well-regarded daily paper which is known for the accuracy of its information, was silent for a while, but at last spoke out, saying that Dr Proudie would be chosen.

And so it was. Just a month after the old bishop's death, Dr Proudie became Bishop of Barchester.

There was a home for elderly men in Barchester, called Hiram's Hospital. Previously Mr Harding had been warden of the home, and he had greatly enjoyed his duties there. But when there were accusations in the newspapers, including *The Jupiter*, that the large income he received could more usefully be spent on the old men themselves, he had given up the post, and become vicar of a small church in the city. Modest man that he was, his one desire was to do what was right, and to avoid any publicity.

However, his family and friends were very angry that he had been unjustly accused, and public discussion of the wardenship became so heated that the government had to take action. Consequently a law was passed, stating that the warden's income should be £450 a year, and that it was the bishop's duty to appoint the warden; Mr Harding's name was not mentioned.

Mr Harding had two daughters. The elder, Susan, was

The new bishop

married to the archdeacon, and Mr Harding spent much of his time with his younger daughter, Eleanor. She had fallen in love with and married a young man called John Bold, but only two years after their marriage, he had become ill and died. For weeks after he was gone, the idea of future happiness in this world was hateful to the young widow; tears and sleep were her only relief. But when she realized she was pregnant, she regained her interest in life, and when her son was born, eight months after his father's death, her joy was inexpressible.

The baby, young Johnny, was all that could be desired. 'Is he not delightful?' Eleanor would say to Mr Harding, looking up from her knees in front of her child, her beautiful eyes wet with soft tears, and naturally he would agree with her.

The baby really was delightful; he took his food eagerly, waved his toes joyfully in the air whenever his legs were uncovered, and did not scream. These are supposed to be the strongest points of baby perfection, and in all these our baby was excellent.

It should not be thought that Eleanor ever forgot her dead husband; she kept his memory fresh in her heart. But yet she was happy with her baby. It was wonderful to feel that a human being existed who owed everything to her, whose needs could all be satisfied by her, whose little heart would first love her and her only, and whose childish tongue would make its first effort in calling her by the sweetest name a woman can hear. And so her feelings became calmer, and she began a mother's duties eagerly and gratefully.

John Bold had left his widow everything that he possessed, and, with an income of a thousand pounds a year, Eleanor felt comparatively rich. John's sister, Mary, came to live with Eleanor, to help take care of baby Johnny. Eleanor had hoped her father, Mr Harding, would also come to live in her house, but he refused, saying that he was quite happy in his modest rooms over a shop in Barchester High Street.

The new bishop, Dr Proudie, was a man who was well aware of his own importance. He considered he was born to move in high circles, and circumstances certainly supported his opinion so far. For some years he had lived in London, where he had been chaplain to the Queen's officers. This high connection and his own natural gifts recommended him to persons in power. Liberal ideas were beginning to take hold of the country as a whole, and as a liberal clergyman, Dr Proudie was involved in various changes in religious matters. His name began to appear in the newspapers, and he became known as a useful and rising churchman. Although he was not a man of great intelligence, and did not even have much business sense, he added a certain weight to the meetings he attended, and his presence at them was generally appreciated.

During this period, he had never doubted his own powers, but always looked forward patiently to the day when he himself would give the orders, while lesser people obeyed. Now his reward and his time had come. He was an ambitious man, and, with his fashionably open-minded views, was not prepared to bury himself at Barchester as the old bishop had done. No! London would still be his ground, for some of the year, at least. How else could he keep himself in the public eye, how else give the government, in all religious matters, the full benefit of his wise advice?

In person Dr Proudie was a good-looking man, smartly dressed, but perhaps a little below medium height. People may

The new bishop

have thought him fortunate in becoming Bishop of Barchester, but he still had his cares. He had a large family, of whom the three eldest were grown-up daughters, and he had a wife. No one dared breathe a word against Mrs Proudie, but she did not appear to add much to her husband's happiness. The truth was that in all domestic matters she ruled over her husband. But she was not satisfied with making the decisions at home, and tried to stretch her power over all his movements, even involving herself in spiritual matters. In other words, the bishop was henpecked.

Mrs Grantly, the archdeacon's wife, in her happy home at Plumstead, knew how to give orders, but in a pleasant and ladylike way. She never brought shame to her husband; her voice was never loud or her looks sharp. Doubtless she valued power, but she understood the limits of a woman's influence.

Not so Mrs Proudie. It was this lady's habit to give the sharpest of orders to everybody, including her husband, even in public. Successful as he had been in the eyes of the world, it seemed that in the eyes of his wife he was never right. All hope of defending himself had long passed; indeed, he was aware that instant obedience produced the closest to peace which his home could ever achieve.

Mrs Proudie was in her own way a religious woman, and one of her strongest beliefs was the need to keep Sunday completely separate from the other days of the week. During the week her daughters were permitted to wear low-cut dresses and attend evening parties, always accompanied by their mother. But on Sunday they had to pay for these sins, by going to church three times and listening to lengthy evening prayers read by herself. Unfortunately for those under her roof who had no such weekday pleasures as low-cut dresses and evening parties to pay for, namely her servants and her husband, strict observance of Sunday duties included everybody.

In these religious matters Mrs Proudie allowed herself to be guided by a young clergyman, Mr Slope. So, because Dr Proudie was guided by his wife, Mr Slope had, through Mrs Proudie, gained a good deal of control over Dr Proudie's religious thinking. When Dr Proudie was appointed Bishop of Barchester, Mr Slope was happy to give up his post as vicar in a poor part of London, to become chaplain to the bishop.

Obadiah Slope and Mrs Proudie shared similar religious beliefs; their relationship was close and their conversations confidential. Mr Slope had regularly visited the Proudies' London home and knew the Misses Proudie well. It was no more than natural that his heart should discover some softer feeling than friendship for Mrs Proudie's eldest daughter, Olivia, and he made a declaration of affection to her. However, after finding how little money her father would give her on marrying, he withdrew his offer. As soon as it was known that Dr Proudie would become bishop, Mr Slope regretted his earlier caution, and began to look more kindly on Miss Proudie again. But he had lost his chance; Olivia was too proud to look at him a second time, and, besides, she had another lover showing interest in her. So Mr Slope sighed his lover's sighs without reward, and the two of them soon found it convenient to develop a hatred for each other.

It may seem strange that Mrs Proudie's friendship for the young vicar should remain firm in such circumstances, but to tell the truth, she had known nothing of his relationship with Olivia. Although very fond of him herself, she expected her daughters to make much more impressive marriages.

The new bishop

Mr Slope soon comforted himself with the thought that, as chaplain to the bishop, he might become richer and more powerful than if he had married the bishop's daughter. As he sat in the train, facing Dr and Mrs Proudie as they started their first journey to Barchester, he began to make a plan for his future life. He understood, correctly, that public life would suit the new bishop better than the small details of cathedral business. Therefore, he, Slope, would in effect be Bishop of Barchester. He knew he would have a hard battle to fight, because power would be equally desired by another great mind – Mrs Proudie would also choose to be Bishop of Barchester. He felt confident, however, that he would win in the end.

In appearance he was tall, with large hands and feet, but on the whole his figure was good. His face, however, was the colour of bad-quality beef, and his hair, which was long, straight, and a dull reddish colour, was kept plentifully oiled. His mouth was large, but his lips were thin and bloodless. It was not a pleasant experience to shake his hand, as there was always a cold dampness to his skin. His face usually wore a frown, as if he thought most of the world far too wicked for his care.

A man of courage and above average intelligence, he firmly believed, like Dr Proudie, in simplifying church ceremony, and like Mrs Proudie, in enforcing total respect for Sunday churchgoing. He had excellent powers of self-expression, which were appreciated more by women than by men. A frequent guest in many London homes, he had been admired by the ladies and unwillingly accepted by the men, but he had an oily, unpleasant way with him which did not seem likely to make him popular in Barchester society.

2
Battle begins

It was known that Dr Proudie would have to appoint a warden for Hiram's Hospital, as the new law stated. No one imagined that he had any choice – no one thought for a moment that he could appoint any other man than Mr Harding. Mr Harding himself, without giving the matter much thought, considered it certain that he would return to the warden's pleasant house and garden.

Mr Harding, therefore, had no personal interest in the appointment of Dr Proudie as bishop, and was quite prepared to welcome him to Barchester. After the Proudies' arrival, he and Dr Grantly went to the bishop's palace to introduce themselves.

His lordship was at home, and the visitors were shown into the well-known room, where the good old bishop used to sit. Every piece of furniture was as familiar to them as their own, but they felt like strangers at once. They found Dr Proudie sitting in the old bishop's chair; they found Mr Slope standing where the archdeacon used to stand, but on the sofa they found Mrs Proudie – and to find a *lady* invading the bishop's study was shocking indeed!

There she was, however, and they could only make the best of it. They greeted his lordship, who introduced them to his lady wife. Then Mr Slope presented himself, offering a damp hand to his new enemy, Dr Grantly, who bowed, looked stiff, and wiped his hand with a pocket handkerchief. Mr Slope then descended to the level of the lower clergy, by speaking a few words to Mr Harding, before rejoining the conversation among the higher powers. There were four people in this group, each of whom considered himself or herself the most important person in Barchester; with such a difference of opinion they were not likely to get on pleasantly together.

'Dr Grantly,' said Mrs Proudie with her sweetest smile, 'you live at Plumstead, I believe, a little way out of Barchester. I do hope the distance is not too great for country visiting. I shall be glad to call on Mrs Grantly, as soon as our horses arrive here. At present they are in London, as the bishop still has meetings to attend there – I fear the government cannot do without him! But when the horses do come down, I shall take the earliest opportunity of visiting Mrs Grantly.'

Dr Grantly bowed, and said nothing. He could have bought everything the Proudies owned and returned it to them as a gift, without much feeling the loss; he had provided a pair of horses for his wife's personal use since the day of his marriage.

'Are there arrangements for Sunday schools in the villages around Barchester, Dr Grantly?' asked Mr Slope.

'Oh!' replied the archdeacon casually. 'Whether there is one or not depends on the local vicar's wife and daughters.'

Mr Slope opened his eyes very wide, but was not prepared to give up his darling project. 'I fear there is a great deal of Sunday travelling here. I see from the timetable that there are three trains in and three out every Sunday. Don't you think, Dr Grantly, that a little energy on your part might get rid of this evil?'

'If you can withdraw the passengers, then I imagine the company will withdraw the trains,' replied the archdeacon.

'But surely, Dr Grantly,' said the lady, 'surely, in our position, we should do all we can to stop such wickedness. Don't you think so, Mr Harding?' And she looked meaningfully at him.

Poor Mr Harding was not sure what he thought, and Dr Grantly, determined not to be told what he should do by a bishop's wife, turned his back on the sofa and asked the bishop if he found the palace comfortable. Dr Proudie himself seemed to have nothing to complain of, but Mr Slope gave a long list of repairs that needed to be done, and Mrs Proudie was not slow to add her voice to his. Finally and with great relief Dr Grantly and Mr Harding were able to bring their visit to an end.

'Good heavens!' cried the archdeacon furiously, once they were in the fresh air. Smoke seemed to be coming from under his hat, like an angry cloud.

'I don't think I shall ever like Mr Slope,' said Mr Harding.

'Like him!' shouted the archdeacon. 'How could any living thing like Mr Slope!'

'Nor Mrs Proudie either,' said Mr Harding.

Then the archdeacon forgot himself, and used some very shocking expressions about the lady.

'The bishop seems a quiet enough man,' suggested Mr Harding mildly.

'He's a fool!' cried Dr Grantly. 'He has no real power or intelligence! No, it's that Mr Slope whom we have to deal with. Did you ever see anyone less like a gentleman? Did you hear him telling us what to think and what to do? How dare he!'

And as the two men walked away from the palace, the archdeacon had war in his heart. He was trying to think how Mr Slope could be driven out of Barchester, before his influence over the bishop could do any lasting damage.

The new residents of the bishop's palace felt as much hatred for Dr Grantly as he did for them, and they were also aware there was a battle to be fought.

Battle begins

Mr Slope, however, was better prepared for the attack than the archdeacon. Dr Proudie had told the Barchester clergy that Mr Slope would give the sermon at the cathedral service the next Sunday. On this occasion the bishop took his seat in the cathedral for the first time, and the good people of Barchester crowded into the great building, eager to see their new bishop and hear his chaplain's words of spiritual guidance. All the clergy attended the service too, even the archdeacon.

The service was very well performed. The prayers were respectfully said, and the music was beautifully sung by the best voices in Barchester, carefully trained by Mr Harding himself. Mr Slope rose to speak to his audience. He was listened to with breathless attention and considerable surprise.

Cleverly giving the impression that he was speaking on behalf of the bishop, Mr Slope made it very clear what would be expected from the Barchester clergy from now on. All the habits and customs which were dear to their hearts were held up to scorn. In particular, he explained how unnecessary church music was, and how much more meaningful the words of the church service were, if spoken rather than sung!

The archdeacon and the rest of the clergy could not believe their ears. All their lives they had conducted services in the way they had considered most excellent, and now this young nobody dared to say they had been wrong! But at last Mr Slope sat down. The bishop, who had been the most surprised of them all, and whose hair almost stood on end with terror, gave the final blessing in a shaking voice, and the service was at an end.

Over the next few days there was heated discussion of Mr Slope and his sermon. Against him were the archdeacon and almost all the clergy, who were so furious they decided he should never be allowed to give a sermon in the cathedral again. Poor Mr Harding began to have doubts about the value of church music; he had always been so proud of the singing in the cathedral, but he wondered if that was another thing he would have to give up, like the wardenship of Hiram's Hospital.

Mr Slope was listened to with breathless attention and considerable surprise.

Battle begins

On Mr Slope's side, however, were one or two clergymen who thought it sensible to congratulate the chaplain on his sermon. They included Mr Quiverful, the vicar of Puddingdale, whose wife presented him every year with a fresh proof of her love, increasing his cares and, it is to be hoped, his happiness equally. Who can wonder that a vicar with fourteen living children and only £400 a year should wish to be polite to a Mr Slope? There were also a number of Barchester citizens who thought Mr Slope might be right. For too long the clergy had gone on in their old-fashioned ways; perhaps it was time to introduce some of the religious changes which were shaking up the outside world. This group consisted mostly of ladies; no gentleman could possibly be attracted by Mr Slope.

However, Eleanor Bold and her sister-in-law Mary Bold were not to be counted among these ladies. It was natural for Mr Harding's daughter to be proud of the cathedral's musical tradition, and angry with Mr Slope for criticizing it. And in such matters the widow Bold and her sister-in-law were in perfect agreement.

But Mr Slope himself persuaded them to think better of him. To their great surprise and no little fear, he came to call on them two weeks after his sermon. The great enemy of all that was good in Barchester entered their own sitting room, and they had no strong arm at hand for their protection. The widow held her baby tightly in her arms, and Mary Bold stood up ready to die in that baby's defence, if such a sacrifice might become necessary.

This is how Mr Slope was received. But when he left, he was allowed to bless the baby, to take each lady's hand and to depart like a trusted friend. How had he turned dislike into friendship and made his peace with these ladies so quickly?

Mr Slope knew how to flatter and say a soft word in the proper place. If he had understood how to charm men as well as he charmed women, he might have risen to a high position.

The day after this visit Eleanor told her father of it, and expressed an opinion that Mr Slope was not quite as black as he had been painted. Mr Harding said little; he did not approve of the visit, but it was not his custom to speak evil of anyone. Instead he turned the conversation to the wardenship of Hiram's Hospital; he told Eleanor he expected the bishop to offer it to him, although at a reduced salary. It was annoying to have to accept the post as a gift from the bishop, especially if it came from the hands of the hated Slope, but he would certainly accept it. Eleanor was delighted at the thought of seeing her dear father happy in his old place at Hiram's Hospital again.

Three months passed, and several changes were made in Barchester. Among other things, absentee clergymen had been recalled to their duties. One of these was Dr Vesey Stanhope, who was quite a stranger in the city. Twelve years ago he had gone to Italy to cure a sore throat, and that sore throat, although it never developed into anything serious, had enabled him to live there in comfortable idleness, while he paid junior clergymen to do his work at home. But when he received an almost threatening letter from Mr Slope, Dr Stanhope realized he would have to spend the summer months, at least, in his house in Barchester, otherwise his income from the Church might be discontinued.

So he and his charming but heartless family took up residence again in Barchester. His wife was still a handsome woman, even at fifty-five. She never appeared until between three and four in the afternoon, but when she did appear, she appeared at her best.

Battle begins

Her dress was always perfect, but she had no other purpose in life than to dress well. Her elder daughter Charlotte, at thirty-five, was a fine young woman, who had taken all the cares of running the house off her mother's shoulders. She and she alone could persuade her father to consider worldly matters. She and she alone could control the foolishness of her brother and sister. She and she alone prevented the whole family from losing their good name and falling into beggary.

Dr Stanhope's younger daughter, Madeline, was a great beauty. She had spent her youth in Italy, where she had destroyed the hearts of many young men without once losing her own, although her reputation had suffered slightly as a result of these adventures. Why she had decided to marry Paulo Neroni, a man of no birth and no fortune, a man of evil temper and oily manners, was a mystery, but perhaps when the moment came, she had no choice. Six months after her marriage, however, she arrived at her father's house in Milan, a cripple and a mother.

She had fallen, she said, and injured her knee, so that she was unable to walk normally. She had therefore made up her mind, once and for ever, that she would never attempt to move herself again. Soon people were saying that she owed her accident to her husband's violence, but she spoke little of Paulo Neroni, except to make it clear he was to be seen and heard of no more. The Stanhopes welcomed the unfortunate beauty and her small daughter into the family home.

Although forced to give up all movement in the world, Signora Neroni had no intention of giving up the world itself. She made arrangements to be carried to the theatres and parties she wished to attend. There, lying on a sofa, she would soon draw every interesting young man to her side by the power of her beauty. Her admirers were too blindly in love to see the cruelty, sharp intelligence and desire for power in her lovely eyes.

Her brother, Bertie, had received an excellent education, but was too idle to take up a profession. He was extremely handsome, with a long silky beard and clear blue eyes, and was continually declaring his love to ladies who pleased him, but, like Madeline, he appeared to have no heart to lose himself.

The Stanhopes made their first public appearance at the Proudies' evening reception. This was an impressive event organized by Mr Slope, who invited all the gentlemen and ladies of Barchester and the surrounding villages. Hundreds of guests were expected at the party, and costly preparations were made, in spite of Mrs Proudie's frequent objections to the expense.

On the evening in question, Mrs Proudie welcomed her guests to the palace's fine rooms, and Mr Slope rushed here and there, giving orders to the servants. The bishop kept tripping over a sofa that had been placed near the top of the stairs. One of his daughters told him it was for a lady with no legs, and he was dying of curiosity to see this strange lady.

Soon Madeline's carriage arrived, and she was carried upstairs to the sofa. There she took up her position, lying on a red silk sheet and wearing a close-fitting white dress, with diamond bracelets on her beautiful arms. She was immediately the centre of attention, as she had intended to be.

Bertie Stanhope, who was talking to the bishop, had the idea of moving Madeline's sofa slightly, to give everyone a little more room – he gave it a push and it rushed halfway across the room. Mrs Proudie was standing with Mr Slope in front of Madeline, trying to be sociable, but she was not in the best of tempers; she found that whenever she spoke to the signora, that lady replied by speaking to Mr Slope. Mrs Proudie was just beginning to feel offended, when one of the sofa legs caught itself in her dress and carried part of the skirt away with an unpleasant tearing sound.

Such destruction to a dress would cause passionate anger in any lady, and Mrs Proudie's expression, as she looked at Bertie Stanhope, was hardly human. Bertie, when he saw what he had done, threw himself on one knee before the lady.

'Forgive me, madam, forgive me!' he cried wildly, trying to separate Mrs Proudie's dress from the sofa leg.

'Unhand it, sir!' said Mrs Proudie scornfully.

'It's not me, it's the sofa,' said Bertie, still on his knees.

'Unhand it, sir!' Mrs Proudie almost screamed.

Just then the signora laughed, just loud enough to be heard. Mrs Proudie turned furiously upon her.

'Madam!' she said, her eyes flashing fire.

Madeline stared her full in the face for a moment, and then said to her brother, 'Bertie, you fool, get up.'

By now Mrs Proudie's daughters had arrived, and very soon they accompanied her out of the room to repair the damage to the dress. Meanwhile, Madeline took the opportunity to fascinate and charm Mr Slope. And when Mrs Proudie returned to the reception, she saw him carrying a selection of the most delicate dishes towards the signora's sofa.

'You are not leaving our guests, Mr Slope,' she said.

'Signora Neroni needs her supper, madam,' answered Mr Slope with a bow and a false smile.

'Let her brother take it to her, Mr Slope,' replied Mrs Proudie. Her anger increased when she realized a few minutes later that he had disobeyed her order. 'Such manners I never saw,' she said furiously to herself. 'I cannot and will not permit it.' And she pushed her way through the crowd, following Mr Slope.

When she reached the sofa, she found the guilty pair alone together. The signora was sitting very comfortably, eating her supper, while Mr Slope was leaning over her, making sure she had everything she wanted. Mrs Proudie walked stiffly up to them, stared at them for a moment, and said, 'Mr Slope, his lordship desires your presence in the dining room; you will join him there, if you please.' She moved away like a ship in full sail.

Mr Slope knew the bishop had not asked for him, but he prepared to leave the room, all the same.

'Is she always like this?' the signora asked him.

'Yes, always the same, madam,' said Mrs Proudie, returning. 'Always equally against improper behaviour of any description,' and she marched back through the room again.

The signora could not follow her, but she laughed a long scornful laugh, sending the sound of it ringing after Mrs Proudie. She could not have thought of a better revenge.

Mrs Proudie could not fight back, because she had her guests to attend to. The reception was coming to an end, and the bishop's wife forced a smile as people said their goodbyes, but she was too angry to make it look convincing. And as Madeline Stanhope was carried out by her servants, Mrs Proudie watched her departing figure as if to say, 'If ever you find yourself within these walls again, I'll teach you a lesson you will never forget.'

3
A rich widow

Two days later Mr Harding was called to the palace to discuss the wardenship of Hiram's Hospital with Mr Slope. The chaplain kept the old man waiting for half an hour, and when he did arrive, he behaved just as if he were an important man of business and Mr Harding a young man applying for a job.

'Now, concerning this post of warden,' he began, 'of course you know the income would be very much reduced. In addition, you would be expected to have the house painted inside every seven years and outside every three years. And the duties – well, I believe, if I am correctly informed, there were hardly any duties to speak of in the past.' He gave a scornful laugh. 'Things are a great deal changed, not only in Barchester, Mr Harding, but also in the wider world. Work is now required from every man who receives wages, and new men are needed in the Church, as in other professions. For example, the bishop is anxious to have a Sunday school attached to the Hospital, for the children of the poor, and the teachers would be under your control and care.'

Mr Harding was now getting very angry, which was what Mr Slope wanted. 'And if I disagree with his lordship's views?' the old man asked, as calmly as he could.

'I hope you do not, but if you do, I assume you would feel unable to accept the post.' Mr Slope intended Mr Harding to refuse the appointment, which would then be vacant for a person of his own choosing.

'I shall consult my friends, but you may tell the bishop, Mr Slope, that I shall not accept the wardenship if I find the conditions that you mention are attached to it,' and Mr Harding left the room.

Mr Slope was delighted. He considered he could take Mr Harding's last speech as an absolute refusal of the appointment, and that is what he told the bishop and Mrs Proudie.

The bishop was sorry to hear it, but Mrs Proudie said firmly, 'There is no cause for sorrow. Mr Quiverful is more in need of it, and, as warden, will be much more useful to us.'

'I suppose I had better see Quiverful?' said the chaplain.

'I suppose you had,' said the bishop.

Meanwhile poor Mr Harding was feeling very miserable. He had lost the wardenship a second time, and been insulted by a man young enough to be his son, but that he could put up with. What really made him unhappy was the thought that he belonged to the past, that his efforts were no longer needed or appreciated, that everything he had done might be worthless.

He went first to Eleanor's house, to tell her his troubles, but found that Mr Slope had visited her the day before. The chaplain had made a very different speech to her from the one he had made to her father, full of flattery and heartfelt hopes that Mr Harding would take the wardenship. So she was surprised and disappointed to see her father looking so unhappy, and could not really sympathize with or understand his dislike of Mr Slope.

Mr Harding's next move was to discuss the matter with the archdeacon, so he drove to Plumstead in a hired carriage. Dr Grantly was out, so, while waiting for him, Mr Harding took the opportunity to discuss recent events with his daughter Susan.

'How can Eleanor bear that Mr Slope?' she asked.

'He's a very clever man,' said her father. 'He has made her think he is a good and honest clergyman.'

A rich widow

'Good and honest indeed!' said Susan scornfully. 'I only hope he won't be clever enough to make her forget her position.'

'Good heavens! Do you mean marry him?'

'What is so improbable about it? Of course that would be his plan if he thought he had any chance of success. Eleanor has a thousand pounds a year of her own.'

'But you can't think she likes him, Susan?'

'Why not? She has no one to look after her.'

'But don't *we* look after her?'

'Oh father, how innocent you are! It is to be expected that she will marry again, but she should wait the proper time, and then at least marry a gentleman.'

Now Mr Harding had something else to worry about. To have as a son-in-law, the husband of his favourite child, the only man in the world whom he really disliked, would be a misfortune he felt he could not bear. In fact, if the truth were known, Eleanor had no more idea of marrying Mr Slope than of marrying the bishop. But it was true she had forgiven him his sermon, his pride, and even his shiny face and oily manners, so in time might she not accept him as an admirer? Strangely enough, Mr Slope was innocent of the crime he was being accused of. This man whose eyes were generally so wide open to everything around him had not yet discovered that the young widow was rich as well as beautiful. It was an error which he was soon to correct.

Dr Grantly did not arrive until dinnertime. He was in an excellent mood and explained why, as they sat down to eat.

'It's all agreed,' he said, rubbing his hands joyfully. 'Arabin has accepted! If anyone can get rid of Slope, Arabin can.'

Francis Arabin was an old Oxford friend of Dr Grantly's, a clergyman of the highest reputation, and also a gentleman. He and Mr Slope had been carrying on a long battle on spiritual matters in the letters pages of *The Jupiter* for some months now, and Dr Grantly thought his friend's intelligence and deep religious knowledge would be extremely useful in the fight against the Proudies. Mr Arabin had therefore been offered, and had accepted, the post of vicar of a small church near Plumstead. Dr Grantly was delighted that Arabin would be so near at hand, for advice and support, and amused that Mr Slope would come face to face with his spiritual enemy very soon.

At the end of the meal Mr Harding finally managed to speak of what was worrying him. The archdeacon's response was firm.

'The bishop has no power to appoint a new man as warden, or indeed to make the warden a Sunday school teacher! All of Barchester expects you to return to Hiram's Hospital, and that's what you will do. I tell you what, my friend, I shall see the bishop when he has neither his wife nor his chaplain beside him, and I think you'll find the matter will end with you becoming warden without any conditions whatever. Leave it to me.'

And so the matter was arranged between them. Dr Grantly's good humour continued till bedtime, when, in the privacy of their room, Mrs Grantly gave him her opinion of what Eleanor might do. His face looked stern, and he said, 'If she does, I'll never speak to her again. I won't be connected to such dirt as that,' and he gave a shudder which shook the whole room.

Mr Slope lost no time in visiting Mr Quiverful to ask if he would like to be warden of the Hospital. Mr Quiverful, in giving his enthusiastic reply, happened to mention that Mr Harding might not need the post because his daughter Eleanor had an income of a thousand a year. This unexpected information caused Mr Slope to cut short his visit, and he rode home,

A rich widow

thinking hard. Why should he not marry the widow, and make the thousand pounds a year his own? And then it struck him that perhaps it would be easier to gain her approval, if he did all in his power to help her father become warden, instead of Quiverful.

He was confident he could manage this, although it would involve a complete change of direction, but he knew he must step cautiously. If he quarrelled with the Proudies and was then refused by the widow, he would have lost all his influence and power. He also remembered that Mrs Bold's brother-in-law was his enemy, the archdeacon, and swore he would never bow the knee to that man, not even for a thousand pounds a year.

Another circumstance influenced him. The vision of the signora was continually before his eyes. It would be too much to say Mr Slope was lost in love, but yet he thought he had never seen so beautiful a woman. He had never been so tempted before, and now it was difficult to resist the temptation – it was hard to consider any plan which would require him to give up his special friendship with this lady.

He decided he urgently needed to find out the truth about Mrs Bold's fortune, so he started making enquiries at once. He was not a man who ever let much grass grow under his feet.

About the time that Mr Slope was visiting Mr Quiverful, a discussion took place at Dr Stanhope's house between Charlotte and Bertie about his unwillingness to earn any kind of income. Finally Charlotte said, in her sensible way, 'Well, Bertie, if you won't work, will you marry a wife with money?'

'I won't marry one without any,' he replied. 'But wives with money aren't easy to find nowadays – the vicars pick them all up.'

'And a vicar will pick up Mrs Bold too, if you don't hurry.'

'Whew!' whistled Bertie. 'A widow! With a son!'

'A baby that will very likely die. The lady is very beautiful, and she has a thousand pounds a year.'

'Well, no one can call me unreasonable, and if you'll arrange it all for me, I'll marry the widow.'

Charlotte was just explaining to him that he must court the lady himself, and was praising her beauty, when Madeline was carried into the room by her servants.

'Madeline, I'm going to be married,' Bertie began as soon as the servants had left.

'There's no other foolish thing left that you haven't done,' said Madeline, 'so you are quite right to try that.'

'Well, that's Charlotte's advice to me. But *your* opinion ought to be the best; you have experience to guide you.'

'Yes, I have,' said Madeline in a hard voice. But she looked very sad, and Bertie was sorry that his words had hurt her.

'Charlotte wants me to marry Mrs Bold,' he said. 'She has a thousand a year and a fine baby son.'

'If it's true she has a thousand a year and has ladylike manners, I advise you to marry her,' said Madeline. 'Even *you* aren't fool enough to marry for love. Marriage is a poor bargain for husband or wife. A man should not sacrifice his freedom unless he gets something in return, but a woman generally has no choice – she has no other way of living.'

'But *Bertie* has no other way of living!' said Charlotte.

'Then for heaven's sake let him marry Mrs Bold,' said Madeline, and so it was decided.

Mr Slope's enquiries about the widow's income had determined him to try his hand at courting her. He had therefore attempted to persuade the bishop that the post of warden should be offered to Mr Harding, but matters were more complicated than he had imagined. Mrs Proudie, anxious for her power to be as visible as possible, had already made it clear to Mrs Quiverful that her husband would be appointed warden.

'Ah, my lord,' said Mr Slope, half laughing, 'we shall all be in trouble if the ladies interfere. I only speak, my lord, in your own best interests. As far as personal feelings go, Mrs Proudie is the best friend I have. But still, in my present position, my first duty is to your lordship.' He smiled his most flattering smile.

'I am quite sure of that, Mr Slope,' said the bishop gratefully. 'Do you really think Mr Harding should be the warden?'

'I do, my lord. What has passed between Mrs Proudie and Mrs Quiverful may be a little inconvenient, but I really do not think that should count in a matter of so much importance.'

He left the poor bishop dreadfully undecided, but on the whole almost determined to oppose Mrs Proudie's wishes, which was exactly what Mr Slope was hoping for.

The chaplain then went on to call on Eleanor Bold, who was playing with baby Johnny in her sitting room. When Mr Slope was announced, Eleanor quickly pushed back her long dark hair, which the baby had pulled down from her widow's cap. Mr Slope stopped for a moment in the doorway, realizing at once how lovely she was, and thinking that, even if she had no fortune at all, she would bring comfort and joy to any man's home.

He sat down close to Eleanor and said confidentially, 'May I ask you a simple question, Mrs Bold?'

'Certainly,' she smiled, 'and I shall give you an honest answer.'

'My question is this: is your father really anxious to go back to Hiram's Hospital as warden?'

'Why do you ask me? Why not ask him yourself?'

'My dear Mrs Bold, there are wheels within wheels, which I fear I have little time to explain to you. No one respects your father more than I do, but I doubt if he respects me.' (He certainly did not.) 'I am afraid there is a feeling in Barchester, I will not call it a prejudice, which runs against me, and your father shares this feeling. Can you deny it?'

Eleanor made no answer, and Mr Slope, in the eagerness of his speech, moved his chair a little nearer to hers. 'That is why I cannot ask him this question as I can ask it of you. But you, my dear Mrs Bold, since I came to Barchester, you have allowed me to regard you as a friend.' Eleanor moved her head slightly; it looked more like a shake than a nod, but Mr Slope took no notice of it. 'To you I can speak openly, and express the feelings of my heart. When I spoke to your father about the post of warden, he gave me the impression he would refuse it, and so the bishop, perhaps mistakenly, has offered it to Mr Quiverful.'

'Then, Mr Slope, there is an end of it!' and tears came to Eleanor's lovely eyes and rolled down her face.

Mr Slope would have given much to be allowed to dry those tears, but he knew his moment had not yet come. Instead he promised to do all he could to persuade the bishop to change his mind, his stated purpose being to protect the interests of Mr Harding, whom he so sincerely admired, and to bring greater happiness to Mrs Bold, whom he dared to call his friend. It was indeed a clever and convincing performance.

At the bishop's palace, revolution was stirring. Since his recent conversation with Mr Slope, the bishop knew it was time to be firm with his wife. If he could only defeat her once, he would be a man indeed! So with great daring he went to her private sitting room to speak to her. He found her at her desk, adding up the bills and frowning over all the expense of a bishop's family.

'Excuse me, my dear,' he began. 'If you are free, I wish to speak to you.' Mrs Proudie looked sourly up at him, and his courage failed him. 'But I see you are busy – another time—'

'What is it, bishop?' asked the lady reluctantly.

'It is about the Quiverfuls, my dear. But as you are busy—'

'What about the Quiverfuls? It is perfectly understood that they are to have the hospital. There is no doubt, is there?'

This was the moment when the bishop needed to show his bravery, in order to win the battle. He said, very gently, 'Well, my dear, I just wanted to mention that Mr Slope seems to think Mr Harding should have the post.'

'Mr Slope seems to think!' she said scornfully. 'I hope, my lord, you will not allow yourself to be governed by a chaplain.'

'Certainly not, my dear. Nothing is less probable. But—'

'Nonsense,' said Mrs Proudie rudely. 'Mr Quiverful will be the warden, not Mr Harding. And that's the end of it.'

'I believe you are right, my dear,' said the bishop, creeping back to the safety of his study.

That evening Mr Slope heard from the bishop that Mrs Proudie's orders concerning the wardenship were to be obeyed. He also received a visit, in his room, from the lady of the house herself. She had something very particular to say to him.

'Mr Slope, I must tell you, I did not at all approve of your behaviour with that Italian woman at my reception. Anyone would have thought you were her lover.'

'Good heavens, my dear madam,' said Mr Slope with a look of horror. 'Why, she is a married woman!'

'That is what she calls herself, certainly. Since then you have visited her and sat with her alone. I consider it my duty to warn you, Mr Slope, that that woman is not a suitable companion for an unmarried young clergyman like you.' How Mr Slope hated her at this moment! But she had not finished. 'There is another thing, Mr Slope. You are far too ready to interfere. Kindly do not give the bishop any more guidance at all. If his lordship wants advice, he knows where to look for it.' And she sailed out.

Mr Slope now knew there certainly was not room in Barchester for the energies of both himself and Mrs Proudie; victory over her had become a matter of urgency.

'I consider it my duty to warn you, Mr Slope, that that woman is not a suitable companion for an unmarried young clergyman like you.'

A rich widow

Meanwhile Eleanor had been made aware of her family's concerns about her apparent liking for Mr Slope. When she had innocently mentioned Mr Slope's offer to help her father, Dr Grantly had accused her of betraying the family's interests in making such an unreliable friend, and Eleanor had felt angry that her brother-in-law, and even her dear father, did not respect her judgement. She was all the more annoyed, because she was not quite sure how far she herself trusted Mr Slope.

Perhaps this disagreement with Dr Grantly made her feel a little isolated, and perhaps that feeling of isolation made her more eager than she would normally have been to accept Charlotte's invitation to spend the evening at the Stanhopes' house.

Indeed, when she arrived there, and discovered Mr Slope was also one of the guests, she almost decided to leave at once. But clever Charlotte made her feel at home immediately; Eleanor was introduced to kind old Dr Stanhope, and was smiled on by Madeline. She had no suspicion that Mr Slope was planning to court her; nor did she notice how much time he spent at the signora's side, or even the guilty looks he sent in her direction. For most of the evening she was left alone with Bertie, and the time simply flew by. Bertie did not flatter her, or sigh like a lover, but he was amusing and friendly, yet at the same time respectful. And when he left Eleanor at her own door at one o'clock in the morning, after a delightful walk in the moonlight, she thought he was one of the most charming men she had ever met.

PART TWO: COUNTER-ATTACK

4
A newcomer to Barchester

Francis Arabin was the younger son of a country gentleman from the north of England. He was educated at an excellent school, and then studied at Oxford University. Here he developed his skill in debating, and became known as an intelligent, humorous, and successful speaker. He was almost always able to make the arguments of the opposing team sound unbelievable, and he aimed to win every debate by using both humour and reason.

But his main interest was in religion, and he gave himself completely to the Church. For it he wrote poems, speeches, and sermons, for it he ate and drank and dressed and breathed. Soon he was ordained as a clergyman, and remained in Oxford as a professor of poetry at one of the university colleges.

Now came the moment of his greatest danger. After much thought, Mr Newman, a well-known Oxford clergyman, left the Church of England to join the Church of Rome, and Mr Arabin was strongly tempted to follow him. In order to consider what he should do, Arabin left Oxford for a while and stayed in a quiet little village by the sea, far from the complications of civilized life.

Everything seemed to point to his choosing the Church of Rome. He loved and admired Mr Newman, and was eager to follow in his footsteps. He approved of Rome's strictness. 'How much simpler it would be,' he thought, 'to live under religious laws which are certain, how much easier to recognize sin and therefore avoid it!' And he wanted so much to show God that he believed in Him; what better proof could there be than making the great sacrifice of the religion in which he had been brought up, and which was supposed to provide his income?

At the time, Mr Arabin was a very young man, too confident in his own powers, and with too little respect for the common sense of ordinary people. But it was an ordinary country vicar, in that small village, who made him see that all true religious guidance comes from within the person, and not from laws made by priests. Arabin also realized that by looking for safety and comfort in the Church of Rome, he was running away from the difficult choice between good and evil. He returned to Oxford a humbler, but a better and a happier man.

When he became vicar of St Ewold's, the church near Plumstead, he was about forty and unmarried. He was above medium height, with slightly greying dark hair. He was not handsome, but his face was pleasant to look at, and there was a humorous look in his eyes. He was popular with women, but living in an Oxford college had meant that he could not marry, so he thought of women as pretty, amusing creatures, nothing more.

He came to stay for a month with the Grantlys, because the vicar's house at St Ewold's needed some repairs. After dinner with the archdeacon, his wife, and their daughters, Mr Arabin went up to his bedroom, and sat at the open window looking out at his church, which he could just see in the moonlight beyond the archdeacon's garden. It was a lovely evening, but Francis Arabin felt sad. It had struck him suddenly, when he saw Dr Grantly's charming wife and children and their comfortable house and garden, how alone in the world he was. He had given his whole life to the Church, and now he thought that had been a mistake. He knew he could have had a high position and great wealth, and probably a family to bring him joy, but now it was too late. He was the vicar of a small country church, and that was all.

The following morning Mr Harding and Eleanor arrived at Plumstead to stay there for a few days. Dr Grantly and Mr Arabin were at St Ewold's, and Mr Harding wanted to walk round the garden, so the two sisters naturally fell into conversation. They had never told each other all their secrets, as Mrs Grantly was ten years older than Eleanor, and they did not see each other often. Mrs Grantly did not, therefore, expect Eleanor to talk to her of love, but she was still very anxious to find out whether her sister had any liking for Mr Slope.

It was very easy to turn the conversation to Mr Slope, and Mrs Grantly was soon criticizing him, which she did with her whole heart, and Mrs Bold was defending him almost as eagerly. Eleanor actually disliked the man; she had almost a fear of him, and would have been delighted never to see him again, but somehow she constantly found herself protecting him against what she considered the injustice of his enemies' attacks.

The conversation moved on to the Stanhopes, and Mrs Grantly heard about Eleanor's recent evening with them. Suddenly she realized Mr Slope had also been there.

'What!' she cried in horror. 'Why, Eleanor, he must be very fond of you. He seems to follow you everywhere!'

Even this did not open Eleanor's eyes. She just laughed, and said she thought he found someone else to attract him at the Stanhopes'. And so the sisters parted. Mrs Grantly felt quite convinced that the hated marriage would take place, and Mrs

Bold was just as convinced that the unfortunate chaplain was yet again being unjustly criticized.

The archdeacon was furious when his wife told him, in private, how she feared Eleanor's relationship with Mr Slope was developing. 'I am sorry, my dear,' he said, 'but if she marries that man, I shall not allow either of them within my doors.'

Susan Grantly sighed. 'Well, perhaps it will never happen. I hope, now that Eleanor is here, she will forget her fatal passion.'

Poor Eleanor, who felt no fatal passion for any man, spent a rather dull evening. Mr Arabin did not seem to notice her much, and he and the Grantlys spent all the time after dinner discussing the various local clergymen. Eleanor began to think, on reaching her bedroom that night, that she was getting tired of clergymen and their respectable, boring way of life, and that she would have had a much pleasanter evening with the Stanhopes.

Mr Arabin, on the other hand, had enjoyed his evening; he appreciated not only the well-informed conversation of the Grantlys, but also the sight of Eleanor's very pretty face under her widow's cap. He began to look forward to the rest of his stay at Plumstead, because she would be there for some of the time.

The next day the whole party drove in the archdeacon's carriage to visit the vicar's house at St Ewold's. In the carriage Eleanor found herself opposite Mr Arabin, and was surprised to discover how easy he was to talk to.

Mr Harding told them an old story he had heard from local people that, a long time ago, a priestess had lived at St Ewold's; she was famous for curing the villagers of all kinds of diseases. Mr Arabin declared he would not want the villagers to rely on a priestess these days, but Mrs Grantly disagreed. 'Every church should have its priestess as well as its priest,' she said, smiling.

'I suppose,' suggested Eleanor, 'that in the past the priestess had all the power. Perhaps Mr Arabin thinks that might happen again if St Ewold's had a modern priestess.'

'I think it is safer not to run the risk of it,' laughed Mr Arabin.

'Such accidents do happen,' said Mrs Grantly. 'They say there is a priestess in Barchester who gives the orders in spiritual matters. Perhaps the fear of that is before your eyes, Mr Arabin.'

This amusing conversation came to an end when they arrived at St Ewold's. Soon the archdeacon and his wife were walking all round the house, telling Mr Arabin what repairs and improvements he needed to make, in order to live comfortably. But while the Grantlys were in the dining room, making plans for a larger fireplace, Eleanor and Mr Arabin found themselves in a small upstairs sitting room.

'There is a beautiful view from here,' said Eleanor, looking out at the cathedral, the bishop's palace, and the trees surrounding Hiram's Hospital. 'This will be your study, I imagine?'

'Yes,' he said, joining her at the window, 'I shall have a perfect view of my enemies. I can fire at them very conveniently from here.'

'You clergymen are always thinking of fighting each other!' said Eleanor, half laughing.

'But are we not here to fight? If we have differences of opinion, should we not go into battle? There is no easy path in religion – I have looked for one and did not find it.' He was silent for a moment, thinking of the time when he had so nearly sacrificed his freedom and his intelligence for that easy path.

Eleanor was impressed by his quiet seriousness. She was used to religious discussion, but she realized, with a certain pleasurable excitement, that this newcomer among them was different from the other churchmen she knew. Instead of arguing bitterly about details, he was only interested in the truth, and was searching humbly for it.

They were interrupted by the archdeacon's shouts of 'Arabin! Arabin!' and went to join the Grantlys in the dining room. Dr

'You clergymen are always thinking of fighting each other!'
said Eleanor.

Grantly suggested the whole room should be enlarged, which Mr Arabin considered would be far too expensive.

'But,' said Mrs Grantly with a smile, 'what if the priestess, who will surely arrive here one day, insists on it?'

'Then she must do it herself,' replied Mr Arabin lightly.

And, having done their work, the party returned home to Plumstead, well satisfied with their visit.

The following Sunday Mr Arabin was to give his first sermon at St Ewold's. He, the archdeacon, and Eleanor were to go there for the morning service, have lunch with the local squire, and return to Plumstead after attending the afternoon service.

The squire of Ullathorne, the area of farmland, villages and churches which included St Ewold's, was a gentleman called William Thorne. He was about fifty, single, and more than a little proud of his appearance. But he was prouder still of his family name. He had a great respect for long, unbroken blood-lines, and his own family line stretched back to the eighth or ninth century. He believed firmly that all traditions and customs should be kept exactly as they always had been.

Mr Thorne did not live alone at Ullathorne House. He had a sister, who was ten years older than him, and an even greater believer in tradition. Once when her brother suggested making a small alteration to the front door of their house, she took to her bed and was ill for a week; she would not come downstairs until she received his promise that it would not be changed in her lifetime. She would not have a modern magazine in her sitting room, and she refused to read poems or novels by living writers. She had thought her brother dangerously liberal-minded when he was younger, and was pleased that the passing of the years had shown him the importance of traditional values. Looking back over five or six centuries of English history, as Miss Thorne liked to do, she often found reason to sigh deeply. She imagined that an innocence and a goodness had existed in the past, which were not to be found in her own time. However wrong she was, no one would deny her the sweetness of her soft regrets!

Mr Arabin, Dr Grantly, and Eleanor met Mr and Miss Thorne at the gates of Ullathorne House, and walked to church together. Large numbers of villagers had gathered there, to see their new vicar. In spite of his long experience of public speaking, Mr Arabin felt a little nervous, knowing that he was being compared with the previous vicar. But fortunately most people in the church considered that Arabin did his work well enough, especially as his sermon was only twenty minutes long.

Then came the lunch at Ullathorne House. Miss Thorne took special care of Eleanor, piling cold meat on her plate and filling her glass with wine. 'It's your duty, you know, to support yourself,' she whispered in the young mother's ear. 'There's more than yourself depending on it.'

And then Miss Thorne was very knowledgeable about teeth. Little Johnny Bold had been troubled for the last few days with his first tooth, and Miss Thorne was shocked to find that Eleanor was giving him some dreadfully modern medicine, recommended by one of the local doctors.

'Take care, my dear,' she said, looking very serious, 'that that man doesn't harm your little boy. But then,' speaking more in pity than in anger, 'I don't know which doctor you can trust now. Poor dear old Dr Bumpwell, of course—'

'Why, Miss Thorne, he died when I was a little girl.'

'Indeed, my dear, and a sad day it was for Barchester.'

The archdeacon was enjoying his lunch. He talked to his host

Mr Thorne about farming; while Mr Thorne, thinking it only polite to pay attention to a stranger, tried to talk to Mr Arabin about religious matters. The two conversations ran on together.

'What are you putting on your fields now, Thorne? Is it guano?' asked Dr Grantly.

'Yes, archdeacon, I get it from Bristol. You'll find a lot of Barchester people, Mr Arabin, who come to services at St Ewold's in the summer, if it isn't too hot for them to walk.'

'I'm glad they stayed away today,' said Mr Arabin, smiling, 'as it was my first sermon.'

'Who do you buy it from in Bristol, Thorne?'

'I drove there myself this year, and bought it straight off the ship. I'm afraid, Mr Arabin, that as the evenings get darker, you'll find it difficult to read in the church. I shall send a man to cut off some branches of the trees outside the south window.'

'The morning light is perfect, at least,' said Mr Arabin. And then he and Eleanor took a walk round the garden, while Miss Thorne cut some flowers, and the archdeacon and the squire finished their discussion about the Bristol guano.

At three o'clock they all went to church again. This time the archdeacon gave the sermon, and half an hour later he, Mr Arabin, and Eleanor shook hands with their Ullathorne friends and drove back to Plumstead.

5
Mr Slope on the attack

The next two weeks passed very pleasantly at Plumstead. Eleanor was a delightful house-guest, and Dr and Mrs Grantly seemed to have forgotten her wicked feelings for Mr Slope. Mr Harding walked in the garden and played the piano, and little Johnny had no more trouble with his teeth. And although Mr Arabin was busy with his new duties at St Ewold's, he made sure he spent every evening at Plumstead.

There had also been a dinner party at the Stanhopes', to which Mrs Bold and Mr Arabin were invited. He, like every other man before him, could not resist the charming signora, and spent the whole evening beside her sofa.

'I have never met so much suffering, joined to such perfect beauty and such a clever mind,' he told Eleanor as they drove home in the archdeacon's carriage.

Eleanor by no means liked to hear this praise. It was, however, extremely unjust of her to be angry with Mr Arabin, as she had herself spent a very pleasant evening with Bertie Stanhope, who had not left her side for one moment. She was not in love with Mr Arabin, although she had spent three weeks in the same house as him and they had enjoyed lengthy conversations together. But a woman does not need to be in love to be irritated when a friend or companion appears to find another woman more attractive. 'I thought he had more wisdom than that,' she told herself, as she sat watching her sleeping child, after they had arrived home. 'After all, I believe Mr Stanhope is the pleasanter man of the two.'

Mr Arabin was not in love, either. Nor was Bertie Stanhope, although he was ready to say so. Only the widow's cap which Eleanor still wore prevented him, in case it was thought too soon for a widow to be receiving another proposal of marriage.

Fortunately, Eleanor's annoyance with Mr Arabin did not last long, and soon they were good friends again. They could have been more, if he had respected her intelligence enough to discuss serious matters with her, as he had done in their first real conversation together. With her he was always gently playful. If he had allowed her to share his deepest thoughts and concerns, she might have learnt to love him.

So things went on at Plumstead. However, the matter of the wardenship was still not decided. Following his promise to Mr Harding, the archdeacon had tried to speak privately to the bishop about it, but had not been able to see him.

Luckily, Mr Harding had another friend fighting his battle for him, a friend even more powerful than the archdeacon, and this was Mr Slope. The chaplain thought he had more and more evidence every day to make him believe the widow would accept his marriage proposal. He felt that giving Mr Harding the wardenship would make him, Slope, more likely to be welcomed as a son-in-law. And he had an even stronger reason for his actions. He wanted a wife, and he wanted money, but he wanted power more than either. He had realized he must fight Mrs Proudie, otherwise he would never be able to rise to a higher position. The wardenship was an excellent reason for war.

The bishop, following his wife's orders, had declared Mr Quiverful should be the new warden. So Mr Slope decided to ride over to Puddingdale and interview the vicar at once.

Mr Quiverful was, on the whole, a good, honest, hard-

Mr Slope on the attack

working man, but the difficulties of his daily life had had a bad effect on his spirit and his sense of honour. He was attempting to bring up fourteen children as ladies and gentlemen, on an income which was hardly enough to provide them with food and clothes. He was anxious for bread and meat and anxious to pay his bills, but not as anxious as a richer man might be, to be well respected by all around him. He could not afford such a luxury. Recently he had felt that his brother clergymen, men he had known for twenty years, looked coldly on him since he had shown himself willing to sit at the feet of Mr Slope. He had seen their looks grow colder still, when it was said he was to become the new warden. This was painful to him, but when he thought of his poor wife and children, and the happy, comfortable life they would all have in the warden's house in Barchester, he felt he had no choice.

Mrs Quiverful cared nothing for the frowns of the clergy. In her heart she had no other ambition than that of seeing her husband and children properly fed and dressed – life for her had no other purpose. So she had no patience with her husband when he had spoken of not wishing to accept the post until he was sure Mr Harding had refused it. Fortunately, they had now received a full promise that the post was theirs, not only from Mr Slope, but also from Mrs Proudie. But what if all had been lost? Mrs Quiverful was a happy woman at present, but it took her breath away when she thought of the danger they had been in.

So when she saw the great Mr Slope arrive, she hurried into the kitchen with an anxious, beating heart, and left the two men alone in the sitting room.

It was easy for a man as experienced as Mr Slope to achieve his purpose. By choosing his words carefully, he was able to withdraw the promise he had made to Quiverful, who, although horrified at the thought of losing the post, could do nothing but express his disappointment. Soon Mr Slope was riding back to Barchester, confident that he could now persuade the bishop to give the post to Mr Harding.

As soon as the front door closed behind the visitor, Mrs Quiverful rushed eagerly back to her husband.

'Well, my dear, we are not to have it,' he said, turning a pale, miserable face towards her.

'What!' she cried, with all the anger and deep despair of a mother who has lost a child. 'What! Who says so?'

She sat as silent as death while he told his story. 'And so you have resigned your post?' said she, at last.

'I had no opportunity of accepting it,' he replied sadly. 'I must wait for another post, that's all.'

'Wait! Shall we feed the children by waiting?'

'It's all we can do, my dear. I feel the disappointment more for your sake than my own.'

Mrs Quiverful saw a small hot tear appear in her husband's eye and roll down his tired face. This was too much for her woman's heart. She ran to him and seized him in her arms.

'You are too soft!' she sobbed. 'But you must go at once and see the bishop! He knows nothing of this! Doesn't all the world know that Mrs Proudie is Bishop of Barchester, and Mr Slope is her slave? For some reason that woman sent him here today – to break her promise to us!'

But she could not persuade her husband to take any action at all, and soon she realized she must do something herself. 'What if, after all, Mrs Proudie knows nothing of Mr Slope's visit?' she thought. She decided to call on the bishop's wife immediately.

Mr Slope on the attack

Normally, a visit to the bishop's palace would make her very nervous – she was only a country vicar's wife – but this time, strengthened by her family's needs, she felt confident. She arranged for a local farmer to drive her into Barchester and wait for her, to bring her back. Finally, she took her last half-crown coin from the box where she kept her savings; she would need it to bribe the servants to let her see the lady of the house.

She arrived at the palace door, and was told Mrs Proudie was not at home. 'I must see her,' said Mrs Quiverful firmly, and pressed her half-crown into the servant's hand. In two minutes she was in Mrs Proudie's sitting room, telling her sad story.

Mrs Proudie was in an excellent mood, having just triumphed in another battle. The bishop had received an invitation to spend a couple of days with the archbishop, and greatly desired to accept it. However, not a word in the invitation mentioned Mrs Proudie, so if the bishop went at all, he must go alone. This presented an enormous difficulty. He could not order his bags to be packed, and then simply set off with a servant, casually telling the lady of his heart that he would be back on Saturday. There are men – probably very wicked men – who do such things, and there are women – more like slaves – who put up with them. But Dr and Mrs Proudie were not among them.

So the bishop had spoken to his wife, but it was a short discussion. Those who are married will understand very well how the battle was lost and won; those who are single will never understand it until they learn the lesson which experience alone can give. Mrs Proudie made sure that before she left her lord, she had seen the answer to the invitation written and sealed.

Now, therefore, she was all smiles as she greeted Mrs Quiverful. But her expression became cold and stern when she heard what Mr Slope had done. Asking Mrs Quiverful to wait for her, she marched out of the room. She was extremely angry with her husband, who, as she thought, had broken the promise he had so clearly given her about the hospital, and she was determined to win the battle against him all over again.

Without knocking at the door, she walked quickly into the bishop's study. She found him seated there, with Mr Slope opposite him. Between Dr Proudie's fingers was the very note which he had written to the archbishop in her presence – and it was open! Yes, he had dared to break open the seal which she herself had approved. It was only too clear that the two guilty men were discussing the invitation, even after the matter had already been decided by her! Mr Slope rose from his chair and bowed slightly. He and Mrs Proudie looked each other full in the face, and knew each was face to face with an enemy.

'What is this, bishop, about Mr Quiverful?' said she.

Mr Slope did not allow the bishop to answer, but replied himself. 'I saw Mr Quiverful at Puddingdale this morning, madam. He has abandoned his claim to the hospital, so I have strongly advised his lordship to appoint Mr Harding.'

'Mr Quiverful has not abandoned anything,' said the lady scornfully. 'His lordship has given his word.'

The bishop remained silent. He was eager to win the battle over his old enemy, and yet his courage failed him.

'Perhaps I ought not to interfere,' said Mr Slope, 'but—'

'Certainly you ought not,' said the lady angrily.

'But,' continued Mr Slope smoothly, 'I considered it my duty to advise the bishop that he will not be popular in Barchester if he fails to appoint Mr Harding. And of course the bishop wishes to reward such an honourable man and such a good clergyman

Mr Slope on the attack

as Mr Harding. It is clear that, in the interview I had with Mr Harding, I misunderstood him—'

'And it is equally clear that you have misunderstood Mr Quiverful,' said she, now at the height of her anger. 'What business have you at all with these interviews? Who desired you to go to Puddingdale this morning? Will you answer me, sir?'

There was dead silence in the room. Mr Slope was standing with his hand on the back of a chair, looking very serious and very threatening. Mrs Proudie was standing at the end of the table, and as she spoke she struck her hand on it with an almost manly strength. The bishop was sitting in his armchair, turning his eyes now to his wife, and now to his chaplain, as each went on the attack in turn. How comfortable it would be if they could fight it out between them, so that one should destroy the other, and then he, the bishop, would know whom to obey!

'Will you answer me, sir?' she repeated. 'Who instructed you to call on Mr Quiverful this morning?'

'I think, Mrs Proudie,' said Mr Slope in a low, calm voice, 'that, under all the circumstances, it would be better for me not to answer such a question.'

'Did anyone send you, sir?'

'Mrs Proudie,' said Mr Slope, 'I am aware how much I owe to your kindness, but my duty in this matter is to his lordship, and I can accept no questioning except from him. He has approved of what I have done, and you will excuse me if I say I need no other person's approval.'

What dreadful words these were to Mrs Proudie's ears! It was evident that the bishop was rebelling against her, and she must move speedily to regain control.

'Mr Slope,' she said, slowly and deliberately, 'I will trouble you, if you please, to leave the room. I wish to speak to my lord alone.'

Mr Slope also felt that everything depended on the present interview. If the bishop lost this battle, he would remain a slave for ever. Now was the moment for victory or defeat!

'His lordship asked me here to discuss important cathedral business,' he replied, hoping for support from Dr Proudie. 'My leaving him at the moment is, I fear, impossible.'

'Ungrateful man!' cried Mrs Proudie. 'My lord, will you kindly beg Mr Slope to leave the room?'

My lord scratched his head, but said nothing. This was as much support as Mr Slope had expected.

'My lord,' said the lady, 'is Mr Slope to leave this room, or am I?' Here Mrs Proudie made a false step. She should not have mentioned the possibility of withdrawing from the battlefield. In answer to such a question, the bishop naturally said to himself that, as it was necessary for one of them to leave the room, perhaps it might as well be Mrs Proudie. But he still said nothing.

Mrs Proudie's anger was boiling over. She could not keep her temper as her enemy did, and so she was defeated.

'My lord,' said she, 'am I to receive an answer or not?'

At last he broke his deep silence and declared himself a member of the Slope party. 'Why, my dear,' said he, 'Mr Slope and I are very busy.'

That was all. No more was necessary. He had gone into battle, put up with the heat and dust of the day, met his enemy, and won the victory. How easy success can be!

Mr Slope saw at once how much he had gained, and turned a triumphant look on the lady. Here he was wrong. He should have looked humbly at her, and remembered that this victory

'Why, my dear,' said the bishop, 'Mr Slope and I are very busy.'

would not last long. He could not arrange to divorce the bishop from his wife, he could not be present every moment of the day, he could not interfere in the privacy of the bedroom, when the wife wished 'to speak to my lord alone'.

But for the moment his triumph was complete, and Mrs Proudie left the room. Now the chaplain told the bishop, in plain words, that he must not let his wife interfere in future, and Dr Proudie, after some hesitation, agreed. Like a good child, the bishop received an immediate reward – he was instructed to write another note to the archbishop, this time accepting the invitation. Mr Slope, more careful than the lady, put the note safely in his pocket. He also persuaded the bishop to see Mr Harding, with the intention of offering him the wardenship. And so Mr Slope, far from disappointed with his achievements, left the palace and posted the note with his own hands.

Mrs Proudie returned unwillingly to her sitting room, where Mrs Quiverful was waiting anxiously for her.

'Your husband has been most weak and foolish,' Mrs Proudie said sternly. 'I find I can do little for him in this matter.'

'Oh, Mrs Proudie! Think of my fourteen children!' Not a word did Mrs Quiverful say about herself, but the tears fell fast.

Mrs Proudie was surprised to find that her hard heart was touched, and she promised to do everything in her power to insist on Mr Quiverful's appointment as warden. Mrs Quiverful returned to Puddingdale, not very hopeful, but satisfied that she had done her best.

6
Two men in love

Still feeling triumphant over his defeat of Mrs Proudie, Mr Slope made the next move in the game, by writing the following letter to Mrs Bold. It was the beginning of what he hoped would be a long and tender correspondence.

My dear Mrs Bold,

You will understand that I cannot at present write to your father. I hope the day will soon come when he may trust and respect me as I admire and respect him. But I cannot deny myself the pleasure of informing you that Mr Q. has today, in my presence, resigned any claim he had to the warden's post, which the bishop now intends to offer your father.

Will you kindly ask Mr Harding to call on the bishop on Wednesday or Thursday between ten and one? Perhaps I should say no more – but still I wish you could make your father understand that no conditions will be attached to the post. I, for one, am persuaded that no man could perform his duty more satisfactorily than he did, or than he will do again.

You will see at once that this letter is confidential. But equally, of course, it is for your father's eyes as well, if you wish to show it to him.

I hope my darling little friend Johnny is as strong as ever – dear little boy! Does he still continue to pull down those beautiful long silken curls of yours?

Your friends in Barchester miss you badly, and envy you your stay among the flowers and fields in this unpleasantly hot weather.

Believe me, my dear Mrs Bold, I am yours most sincerely,

Obadiah Slope

This would not have been a bad letter, except for one thing. Gentlemen do not write to ladies about their silken curls, unless they know them very well, but Mr Slope could not be expected to know this. Having finished his letter, he took it to Mrs Bold's house, and left instructions for it to be sent on to Plumstead.

Then he went to visit Signora Neroni. This was, he knew, extremely unwise. Not only was her husband living, so he, Slope, could not court her honestly, but in addition, she had nothing to recommend her as a clergyman's wife; she had no fortune and she was a helpless, hopeless cripple. He knew that by visiting her he might ruin his reputation and his chances with Mrs Bold, but he could not help himself. Passion, for the first time in his life, was too strong for him.

The signora, on the other hand, cared no more for Mr Slope than for the twenty others who had admired her before him. She was like a female spider, who could not live without catching flies – this exercise of power was the one excitement of her life – and Mr Slope was the finest fly that Barchester could offer.

Mr Slope was shown into the sitting room, where she lay in all her beauty on the sofa. He rushed to her side and took her small delicate hand in his large red one, to kiss it tenderly.

'Signora, you are lovelier than the heroines of ancient times!' he cried, with what he thought was his most winning smile.

'That is not very flattering, Mr Slope,' said she. 'Most of them were rather foolish, and gave up all for love. Remember, Mr Slope, whatever you do, never mix love and business.'

Mr Slope was speechless. Had she guessed his intention to court Mrs Bold, and would she now punish him for it?

'Which is it to be, Mr Slope?' she asked sternly. 'Love or money? Take my advice – never mind love. There's no long-

Two men in love

lasting happiness in it. But in wealth, houses, land, yes, in them there is something to be kept and enjoyed for many years.'

'Oh, no,' said Mr Slope, feeling he must protest, 'this world's wealth will make no one happy. We must hope for happiness in heaven, signora!'

'Nonsense! You don't believe that!' And she watched in fascination as her fly struggled to escape.

Mr Slope had no idea how to answer her, but he did his best. 'You like to shock, signora, but your heart is true.'

'My heart! I do not have one. But that does not matter to you, because the courtship you are planning will result in something more solid than such a ghostly love as mine—'

'Your love would satisfy the dreams of a king,' said he, not quite sure what his words meant.

'You mean an archbishop.' Poor man! She was very cruel to him. 'Now, am I to understand you say you love me?'

He had never said so, but he could not possibly deny his love, so down he went on his knees and swore he loved her, and would love her until the end of time.

'And now another question – when are you to be married to my dear friend, Eleanor Bold?'

There was nothing he could say, except, 'Oh signora, how can you insult my feelings for you? My heart is all your own!'

And so the game went on. Mr Slope knew he was insulted, scorned, laughed at, yet he could not tear himself away. He had looked for joy in loving this lovely creature, and found only bitterness. He loved furiously, madly, and passionately, but he had never played the game of love. The signora did not love at all, but she knew every move in the game.

Finally, she offered him her hand again, and he covered it

with kisses. 'Come, forgive me, Mr Slope,' she said with her sweetest smile. 'Shall we be friends again?'

'Oh Madeline, tell me that you love me – do you love me?'

But at that moment Mrs Stanhope entered the room, and soon afterwards Mr Slope said goodbye and left the house, his heart full of confused emotions.

That afternoon the archdeacon and Mr Harding, who were in Barchester on business, collected Eleanor's post from her house, to take back to her. As soon as Dr Grantly saw Mr Slope's letter, he recognized his enemy's handwriting on the envelope. He was very angry indeed, and handed it to Mr Harding with the tips of his fingers, as if it contained poison. The poor father had to give it to Eleanor when they arrived at Plumstead.

Eleanor opened the letter as she was getting dressed for dinner. She was so delighted to find that her father could now become warden again that she did not realize the information should not have come to her from an unmarried young clergyman. As she read on, she was offended by her boy being called Mr Slope's darling, and when she came to the mention of her silken curls, she gave a shudder of disgust. But on the whole she was grateful to Mr Slope for wishing to help her father.

At dinner, however, the whole party looked stern and silent. Dr Grantly had betrayed his sister-in-law by whispering into Mr Arabin's ear before the meal, 'I very much fear Eleanor is to marry Mr Slope!' Mr Arabin had been horrified to hear it, and was now as sorrowful and unsociable as the Grantlys. Eleanor, unaware that Mr Slope's letter had already been much discussed, felt that she had been judged guilty of something, but had no idea what.

Two men in love

After dinner, the ladies went into the sitting room, while the gentlemen stayed at table with their final glass of wine. Dr Grantly had asked his wife to speak to Eleanor about her correspondence with Mr Slope, and so, rather unwillingly, Susan asked her younger sister about the letter. Eleanor, feeling she was being treated like a child, refused to tell Susan what the letter was about, or to show it to her; she became angrier and angrier at her sister's continual questioning. Finally Susan said, with great formality, 'Well, Eleanor, it is my duty to tell you that the archdeacon thinks such a correspondence is disgraceful, and that he cannot allow it to go on in his house.'

Eleanor's eyes flashed fire as she jumped up from her seat. 'You may tell the archdeacon that wherever I am, I shall receive letters from whom I please. If Dr Grantly has used the word "disgraceful", I think he has been ungentlemanly and inhospitable. I shall show the letter to Father, but to no one else.' And she ran upstairs to her bedroom and her baby.

Half an hour later Mr Harding crept up to her room and knocked at the door. Eleanor welcomed him in, and kissed him, and told him she could not put up with the archdeacon's pride and unkindness any longer. She showed him Mr Slope's letter, thinking her father would see immediately what an innocent, well-meaning letter it was. But poor Mr Harding could only see the 'darling boy' and the 'silken curls', and felt sure Dr Grantly's suspicions were correct. It was almost a love-letter, and it meant that Eleanor must be planning to marry the hated Slope. The foolish, weak, loving father did not say one word to her. If he had, Eleanor would have expressed her disgust at the idea of marriage to the chaplain, Mr Harding would have been delighted, the Grantlys would have apologized, and Mr Arabin

– Mr Arabin would have dreamt of Eleanor and woken next morning with ideas of love and plans for marriage.

But all this was not to be. Mr Harding folded the letter, gave it back to her, kissed her, said, 'God bless you, my child!' and crept slowly away to his own room.

Immediately there was another knock at Eleanor's door, and a servant brought a message from the archdeacon, asking if Mrs Bold would mind coming to Dr Grantly's study for two minutes. Eleanor did mind; she was tired and unhappy, but she was not a coward. So she tied on her cap and went downstairs with a beating heart.

The archdeacon started his speech to Eleanor by explaining that he wanted to give her some brotherly advice. She replied coldly that if she needed any advice, she had her father to ask. This made Dr Grantly hesitate, but he went on to ask about Mr Slope's letter. He was quite surprised when Eleanor held it out for him to look at. After reading it, he felt convinced, like Mr Harding, that Eleanor would soon be married to Mr Slope.

'Do you think, Eleanor, this is a suitable letter for you to receive from Mr Slope?'

'I do,' said she angrily, perhaps forgetting the unpleasant matter of the silken curls. 'You think he is a messenger from the devil, just because you disagree with him! *I* think he is doing a great deal for my father and I am grateful to him.'

This was too much for the archdeacon, who burst out, 'Eleanor, is it worthwhile to break away from all those who love you, for the sake of Mr Slope?'

'I don't intend to break away from anybody, Dr Grantly.'

'Eleanor, I must speak out! Mr Slope is altogether beneath you. I beg you, think of this before it is too late!'

Two men in love

'Too late! What do you mean? I don't understand.'

'Ask Susan, or your father, or Mr Arabin—'

'You haven't spoken to Mr Arabin about this!'

'Certainly I have, and he agrees with me and Susan that it is impossible you should be received at Plumstead as Mrs Slope.'

Dr Grantly would never forget the look on Eleanor's face as he said that name. For a moment she could find no words to express her anger and disgust.

'How dare you!' she said at last, and hurried out of the room. When she reached her bedroom, she threw herself on her bed and sobbed as if her heart would break.

She decided to leave Plumstead the following day. She could not stay under the archdeacon's roof a moment longer than necessary, and it was arranged that the carriage would take her back to Barchester after lunch.

Meanwhile Mr Arabin's every waking thought was of Eleanor. As soon as he had heard that another man was carrying off this sweet prize, he began to be very fond of her himself. In fact, he was in love with her, although he did not know it yet, and he rode back from St Ewold's to Plumstead just before lunch, hoping for an opportunity to see her before she left.

He found her alone in the sitting room. She had spent a sleepless night and a miserable morning, and was not at all pleased to see Mr Arabin, whom she blamed for supporting the archdeacon in his unjust attacks on Mr Slope.

'I am sorry our pleasant time together is over so soon, Mrs Bold—' he began nervously.

'It is a pity, certainly, that people do so much to destroy the pleasantness of their days,' she said, interrupting him. 'You should practise what the Church teaches us, Mr Arabin.'

'Undoubtedly I should. Have you any special reason for telling me this, Mrs Bold?'

'You advised Dr Grantly concerning my – friendship – with Mr Slope,' she replied in a terribly calm voice. 'Just because I have treated that gentleman with politeness, you and Dr Grantly assume I am to marry him – something no reasonable person would consider possible. Your accusation is simply designed to make me hate this enemy of yours, that's all.'

She turned her back on him and walked out into the garden. Mr Arabin was left in the room, counting the squares in the pattern of the carpet. He was dreadfully unhappy at the hard words he had received, and yet happy, wonderfully happy, at the thought that, after all, the woman whom he so much admired was not to become the wife of the man whom he so much disliked. At last he was aware that he was in love. Forty years had passed over his head, and so far woman's beauty had never given him an uneasy moment. His present moment was very uneasy.

But only a few minutes later he went out into the garden to court her as well as he could. He found her under a large tree.

'I hope we are not to part as enemies?' said he.

'I try not to have enemies,' said Eleanor, 'but people must be respected if they are to be friends.' She was very angry with him for considering her judgement to be so poor and her character to be so weak that she could possibly marry Mr Slope.

'And am I not respected?'

'*You* did not respect *me* if you spoke of me as that man's future wife. I was deceived; I believed you thought well of me.'

'Thought well of you!' he cried. 'I must use stronger words than those. I respect and admire you, as I have never respected or admired any woman.'

Two men in love

And he walked beside her, struggling to express his feelings. Eleanor was determined to give him no assistance. Poor Mr Arabin! The words in his heart were, 'Since you do not love that other man, and are not to be his wife, can you love me, will you be my wife?' But with all his experience of public speaking in colleges, churches, and cathedrals, now, when he most needed to speak persuasively, the words would not come.

And yet Eleanor understood him as completely as if he had declared his passion like a practised lover. She felt a sort of joy in knowing that his heart belonged to her, but he had offended her deeply and she could not bring herself to abandon revenge just yet. She was flattered, but not ready to accept his courtship.

'Answer me this one question,' said Mr Arabin suddenly, stepping forward and turning to face his companion. 'You do not love Mr Slope? You do not intend to be his wife?'

This made Eleanor angry all over again, just at the moment when she had been feeling softer towards him. 'I shall answer no such question,' she said sharply, 'and what's more, I must tell you that you have no right to ask it. Good morning!'

And she walked proudly away from him, back into the house, where she had lunch with her father and sister. Half an hour later she was in the carriage, leaving Plumstead without seeing Mr Arabin again.

His walk was long and sad, among the dark trees at the end of the garden. To his ears, her last words meant the end of their friendship. He knew so little of women! He could not understand that Eleanor might be furious with him and yet love him.

Victory for Mrs Proudie

When Eleanor arrived at her house in Barchester, she was met by her sister-in-law, who ran out to greet her, saying, 'Oh Eleanor, have you heard what has happened? The poor dean, Dr Trefoil, is very ill – I fear he is dying!'

The news spread fast all round the city, and most of the clergy were gathering in the cathedral library. This was a large room which was attached to the dean's house – a convenient place to wait for information about his state of health. It appeared that the old man had suddenly fallen ill, and was close to death. The great London doctor, Sir Omicron Pie, had been sent for, but meanwhile the Barchester doctors were doing their best.

In the library the clergy spoke in low, respectful voices.

'He was an excellent, sweet-tempered man,' said a vicar.

'It will be hard to replace him,' said another. 'Archdeacon, I hope the government will not appoint a stranger to the post.'

'We will not talk of a new dean,' said Dr Grantly, 'while there is yet hope that Dr Trefoil may live.'

'Oh no, of course not. Still, there is no one who has more influence with the present government than Mr Slope—'

'Mr Slope!' said two or three voices together. 'Mr Slope – Dean of Barchester! Impossible!'

The archdeacon had turned pale. What if Mr Slope should become Dean of Barchester? There was no reason for it at all, but the man seemed to have power over Dr Proudie, and Dr Proudie had won the prime minister's approval.

'I imagine such a thing is out of the question,' he said, 'but

Victory for Mrs Proudie

at the moment I am thinking more of our poor friend than of Mr Slope.'

'Of course, of course,' said the first vicar, 'so are we all. Poor Dr Trefoil, the best of men, but—'

'It's the most comfortable dean's residence in the country,' said another.

'And two thousand pounds a year,' said a third.

'No, it was cut down to twelve hundred,' said the first.

'I think you'll find it's fifteen hundred,' said a fourth.

'What do you say, Grantly?' asked the first speaker.

'Twelve,' replied the archdeacon firmly, putting a stop to all discussion of the dean's income.

The bishop was sitting in his study at the palace when he heard the news of the dean's illness. Dr Proudie was not feeling well himself. It was only yesterday that he had won his first battle against Mrs Proudie, and had thought his slavery might be at an end. He had spent a happy evening with Mr Slope, planning many things in his new-found freedom, but as the bed-time hour approached, his heart sank within him. Could he trust himself to come down to breakfast a free man? Unwillingly he climbed upstairs, an hour later than usual, to the room he shared with his lady wife. What passed between them that night cannot be easily described. It is enough to say that he came down the following morning a sad and thoughtful man, looking thinner, older and greyer than before. All ambition was now dead within him.

When Mr Slope heard the news, it occurred to him that he himself might be the new dean. He too wondered if the income would be twelve hundred, fifteen hundred, or two thousand, but in any case it would be a great step forward for him – he would have more power than the archdeacon.

He began to make his plans. First, he was sure he could rely on the bishop's support – the prime minister might ask Dr Proudie's advice on who should fill the vacancy. Secondly, he knew a gentleman, Sir Nicholas Fitzwhiggin, who was an inspector of schools, and who had many friends in the government – he hoped Sir Nicholas would use his personal contacts to help him. And finally, he flattered himself that he had a useful friend in Mr Towers, a journalist on *The Jupiter*, who would be able to put forward the name of Slope in the newspaper's columns.

The dean was still alive, but Mr Slope did not want to waste any time. So he went straight to the bishop's study, knowing that Dr Proudie was to set out the next day for the archbishop's palace. The bishop was sitting in his chair, doing nothing and thinking of nothing, as Mr Slope entered.

'Well, Slope?' said the bishop somewhat impatiently. He was not anxious to have much conversation with Mr Slope.

'Your lordship will be sorry to hear that the poor dean's health has not improved at all.'

'Oh – ah – hasn't it? Poor man! Poor man!'

'It will naturally be important to your lordship to have, as the new dean, a man who shares your views. If I might be allowed to advise, I would suggest you discuss this with the archbishop tomorrow. I have no doubt that your wishes, supported by the archbishop, would carry much weight with the prime minister.'

'The prime minister has always been kind to me, very kind. But I am unwilling to interfere in such matters, unless asked. And indeed, if asked, I don't know whom I should recommend.'

This was a slight shock to Mr Slope, who, however, recovered quickly. His difficulty was how to make his speech sound modest

Victory for Mrs Proudie

enough. 'Perhaps I can help you there, my lord. I have been considering the matter for some time, and if poor Dr Trefoil must go, I do not see why, with your lordship's assistance, I should not hold the post myself.'

'You!' cried the bishop, in a far from flattering manner.

The ice was now broken, and Mr Slope began to speak smoothly and persuasively. He talked of his achievements so far, his work for the Church, his friends in high places, and his great respect and admiration for Dr Proudie. He described the ways he, as dean, could add to Dr Proudie's comfort in Barchester and influence over the clergy. Then, without pausing, he produced another seven or eight reasons why no one on earth could make such a good Dean of Barchester as himself.

The bishop sat there, speechless. He would never have imagined Mr Slope as Dean of Barchester, but little by little he began to see there would be advantages for himself in this promotion. He could well do without Mr Slope, who was no longer useful to him in his war against Mrs Proudie; in this war the bishop had now admitted defeat. If, indeed, he could have slept in his chaplain's bedroom instead of his wife's, there might have been some reason to keep Mr Slope.

So, in the end, the bishop approved of Mr Slope's suggestion, and it was decided that he would mention it to the archbishop as soon as the occasion presented itself. But Dr Proudie wanted something from his chaplain in return. 'About Hiram's Hospital,' he said. 'I think, on the whole, it will be better to let Mr Quiverful have it. He has a large family, and is very poor.'

'But, my lord,' said Mr Slope, not wanting to let Mrs Proudie gain a victory, 'I am really much afraid—'

'Remember, Mr Slope,' said the bishop, 'I cannot promise you the post of dean. I will speak to the archbishop, as you wish, but I cannot be sure—'

'Well, my lord,' said Mr Slope, fully understanding the bishop, 'perhaps you are right about Mr Quiverful. I can easily manage matters with Mr Harding. Leave him to me.'

'Yes, Slope, that will be best, and you may be sure that I will do anything I can to put forward your name.'

And so they parted. Mr Slope now had much business on his hands. He had to make his daily visit to the signora. It would have been wiser not to do this, but passion had made him blind. He decided he would take tea at the Stanhopes' just this once,

Mr Slope, along with many others, thought that all was fair in love and war.

and then go there no more. He also had to arrange matters with Mrs Bold. She would make as charming a dean's wife as a chaplain's, and her fortune would be a useful addition if the dean's income was found to be only twelve hundred.

Mr Slope, along with many others, thought that all was fair in love and war. So he had not considered it dishonourable to bribe and flatter Eleanor's young maid, in order to get information from her about the widow. In this way he had heard about the arrival of his letter at Plumstead and the arguments which had followed; to his delight, the maid thought she had heard Mrs Bold declare that she 'wouldn't give up Mr Slope for anybody'. This made the chaplain feel quite certain that the beautiful widow would now, in all probability, accept his offer. He must, therefore, make his declaration very soon, before it was known that Mr Quiverful, not Mr Harding, was to have the wardenship.

In addition, he had to gain the support of Sir Nicholas and Mr Towers, in order to become dean, so he sat down at once to write to each gentleman. Once he had posted the letters, he was free to sit by the lovely signora's sofa for the rest of the evening.

During the next week, Mrs Bold spent a great deal of time with the Stanhopes, of whom she became fonder and fonder. If asked, she would have said Charlotte was her special friend, but she liked Bertie nearly as much. She allowed him a kind of familiarity which she had never known with anyone else, and which she did not realize could be dangerous. In all this she was perfectly innocent, having no idea of him as a lover. But every familiarity into which Eleanor was trapped was deliberately planned by Charlotte. The sister knew well how to play her game, and played it without mercy; she knew her brother's character, and yet she would have handed over to him the young widow, and the young widow's money, without pity or regret. In order to do this Charlotte made her family and her father's house very welcoming to Mrs Bold. There was a lack of formality about them all which Eleanor found refreshing, after the priestly pride and stiffness she had recently had to put up with.

But Eleanor by no means forgot Mr Arabin. She had parted from him in anger, and she was still angry with him, but she sincerely wanted to meet him again, and forgive him for his sins towards her. The words he had spoken still sounded in her ears. She knew that they meant he loved her, and if he ever did make a declaration of love, she thought she might receive it kindly. But first he would have to confess that he had misjudged her.

She would see him again at Miss Thorne's garden party in a week's time. This was a grand event with lunch and all kinds of entertainment – sports and games, music and dancing. Everyone for miles around was looking forward to it.

The Grantlys had, of course, been invited to the party, and Eleanor had originally intended to go to Ullathorne with her sister. But because of her quarrel with the archdeacon, she had decided to go with the Stanhopes. However, she was alarmed to find that Mr Slope would be accompanying the Stanhopes, and annoyed to discover that she would be sharing a carriage with him. She hated the thought of Mr Arabin seeing her get out of the same carriage as Mr Slope, but could think of no way of avoiding the situation.

The bishop returned from his stay with the archbishop the day before the garden party. On his arrival he crept into his palace with beating heart; he had stayed three days longer than

Victory for Mrs Proudie

planned, and feared he would be punished for it. Nothing, however, could be more welcoming than the greeting he received; his daughters kissed him, and Mrs Proudie held him in her arms, calling him her dear, darling, good little bishop. This was a very pleasant surprise.

Mrs Proudie had changed her behaviour towards her lord. She wanted to show him that if he obeyed her, he would get his reward. Mr Slope had no chance of winning against her; not only could she half kill the poor bishop with her midnight anger, but she could comfort and cheer him with good dinners, warm fires, and an easy life.

She sat down with him in his study. The bishop felt delightfully relaxed, in his favourite armchair in front of the fire.

'I hope you enjoyed yourself at the archbishop's,' she began, with her best attempt at a loving smile.

'Oh yes, my dear. The archbishop was quite polite to me.'

'I'm delighted to hear it.' She changed the conversation. 'Well, the poor dean is still alive. Was it discussed at the palace?'

'Was what discussed?' asked the bishop.

'Replacing the dean,' said Mrs Proudie. As she spoke, her eyes flashed in their old familiar way, and the bishop felt a little less comfortable than before.

'Hardly at all, my dear. It was just mentioned.'

'And what did you say about it, bishop?'

'I? Oh, I just said – I thought – that is, if the dean—' As he searched for the right words, he saw his wife looking sternly at him, and he began to wonder. Why should he suffer so much to assist a man like Slope? Why fight a losing battle for a chaplain? From that moment he decided to give up his support for Slope, and try to gain his wife's approval in everything he did.

'I am told,' said Mrs Proudie, speaking very slowly, 'that Mr Slope hopes to be the new dean.'

'Yes – certainly, I believe he does.'

'I hope, bishop, that you did not do anything so foolish as to mention his name to the archbishop.'

'Well, my dear, I may have done—'

'What were you thinking of, bishop? A man who hardly knows who his own father was! A man I found without bread to eat or a coat on his back! Dean of Barchester, indeed! I'll dean him!'

'But my dear, I thought you were beginning to dislike Mr Slope, and therefore, it seemed to me that if he got this post, and stopped being my chaplain, you might be pleased.'

Mrs Proudie laughed a loud, scornful laugh. 'Of course he'll stop being your chaplain! I couldn't for a moment think of living in the same house as such a man. But he won't become dean, oh no! I have my eye on him. It wasn't enough for him to interfere in cathedral business, to get you, my dear, into trouble and cause quarrelling among the clergy, no, that wasn't enough for him! He is now behaving in a most disgraceful way with that Italian woman. I shall show Mr Slope to the world for what he is – a false, mean, wicked man. Dean, indeed! The man has gone mad!'

The bishop said nothing further to excuse himself or his chaplain, and he and his wife went in to dinner. That evening was the pleasantest he had spent in his own house for a long time. And in the morning, when he was dressing for the Ullathorne party, he promised himself he would never again go into battle against a fighter so skilled and so deadly as Mrs Proudie.

PART THREE: PEACE RETURNS

8
The garden party

The day of the Ullathorne party arrived, and Miss Thorne was in great anxiety about the preparations. Mr Thorne also had a great deal to do. But the most hard-working, the most anxious and the most effective person at Ullathorne House was the steward, Mr Plomacy. In his youth he had lived through dangerous times, and had once been sent over to Paris with secret letters, hidden in his boot, for the King of France. He had been lucky enough to return safely, and since then had stayed quietly at home, but the adventure had gained him a reputation for political cleverness and complete reliability. Now he had been steward of Ullathorne for more than fifty years, and it had been a very easy life. Who could require much work from a man who had carried documents which, if discovered, would have cost him his head?

But on occasions such as this, Mr Plomacy proved his real worth. He had the honour of the family at heart, and he appreciated the duties of hospitality for such an ancient house. Therefore he always took the arrangements for such events into his own hands, and very well he managed them, too.

The day had been planned as follows: the guests would gather in the house and garden; sports would be played in the field; a generous meal would be served. Two enormous tents had been set up, one in the main part of the garden, near the house, and the other in the sports field, separated from the garden by a stream. High society – the lords, ladies, clergy, and gentlemen of the surrounding area – would have their lunch in the garden tent, while low society – the farmers, shopkeepers, and other ordinary working people – would eat in the field tent.

A difficult question presented itself immediately. Who, exactly, was to be fed in the garden and who in the field? It was easy to see that Bishop Proudie would belong in the garden, and Farmer Greenacre, with his red face and plain country manners, in the field. But what about Mrs Lookaloft, whose husband was only a farmer, but whose daughters attended a fashionable private school, and who had a piano in her sitting room? She would not be happy talking about butter and chickens to her neighbour Mrs Greenacre, and yet she was no fit companion for the Thornes and Grantlys. People like her would certainly want to leave the field and cross the stream to join high society in the garden tent, if they could. All Miss Thorne and Mr Plomacy could do was to make their arrangements and hope for the best.

It was a beautiful sunny day, and soon the farm workers and townspeople began to pour in through the gates. Mr Plomacy wanted to turn away all those who had no invitation, but Miss Thorne insisted on offering her hospitality to everybody.

Some ladies and gentlemen arrived, and were shown into the main sitting room in the house. Then, as Miss Thorne had feared, Mrs Lookaloft and her adult daughters marched confidently into the room. Miss Thorne's servants knew the Lookalofts had no right to be there, but did not like to prevent them entering. Miss Thorne herself, although shuddering slightly at the sight of their unsuitably low-cut dresses, greeted them politely, if a little coldly.

Mr Arabin had also arrived, just in time to see the Stanhopes' carriage stop in front of the house. He watched in disgust as Mr Slope handed Mrs Bold out of the carriage. The next to arrive

The garden party

Mr Arabin watched in disgust as Mr Slope handed Mrs Bold out of the carriage.

were the Proudies, followed by all the important Barchester families, and soon the house and gardens were full of noise and movement.

Eleanor left the Stanhopes as soon as possible, and went to look for her father. She was pleased to find him with Mr Arabin. There was something particular she wanted them both to hear.

'I came with the Stanhopes, father,' she said. She saw Mr Arabin looking at her sternly. She knew his accusation was: 'You came with them in order to be accompanied by Mr Slope.'

She continued rather breathlessly, 'In our carriage were Dr Stanhope, Charlotte, myself, and Mr Slope.' As she spoke the last name, Mr Arabin turned and walked slowly away. 'Father,' she said desperately, 'I couldn't help coming with Mr Slope!'

'Why would you wish to help it, my dear?'

'Father, you must know all the things they said at Plumstead. How unjust the archdeacon was, and Mr Arabin too! He's a hateful man, but—'

'Who's a hateful man, my dear? Mr Arabin?'

'No, father, you know I mean Mr Slope. He's the most hateful man I ever met in my life. But how could I help coming in the same carriage as him?'

A great weight began to roll off Mr Harding's mind. So, after all, the Grantlys, with all their wisdom, were wrong! His Eleanor, the daughter of whom he was so proud, was not to become Mr Slope's wife! 'My darling girl, I am so delighted!'

'But surely, father, *you* didn't suspect—'

'I don't know what you mean by "suspect", Eleanor. There would be nothing disgraceful in such a marriage.'

And Mr Harding would have explained that Mr Slope was a very good sort of man and a very suitable second husband for

The garden party

a young widow, if he had not been interrupted by Eleanor's greater energy.

'It *would* be disgraceful! It would be wrong! It would be horrible! I don't wonder at Dr Grantly and Susan, but father, I do wonder at *you*. How could you believe it of me?' And Eleanor, unable to hold back her tears, sobbed bitterly.

But she could not be angry for long with her father, who confessed his misjudgement of her character and promised never to make the same mistake again. He helped her dry her tears, and, arm in arm, in perfect happiness, they walked towards the house.

Miss Thorne was at her front door, welcoming latecomers. The signora, looking as beautiful and fascinating as ever, was carried inside and placed carefully on a sofa, where, as usual, she was the centre of male attention. But soon all eyes turned to the door again, and Lady de Courcy made her entrance.

Lady de Courcy had chosen to show that she was socially above everyone else by arriving three hours late, then complaining loudly of the poor quality of the country roads. But she found a companion to her liking in the bishop's wife, and soon the two ladies discovered they thought alike on many matters.

'Charming person, Miss Thorne!' said Mrs Proudie.

'Charming, indeed! And isn't her dress delightful?'

'Quite delightful. I wonder if she paints – there's something about the colour that makes me think—'

'I have no doubt she does. But tell me, Mrs Proudie, who is that woman on the sofa by the window?' And Lady de Courcy looked meaningfully over at the signora.

'She's the dreadful Italian woman, Lady de Courcy. You must have heard of her.'

'What Italian woman? Tell me more, I beg you!'

'She's not absolutely Italian. She calls herself Signora Neroni, but in fact she's Dr Stanhope's younger daughter.'

'Ah-h-h-h! I've heard my son George mention her. He heard a lot of stories about her in Rome.'

'She made her way into my house once, before I knew anything about her, and I cannot tell you how disgraceful her behaviour was – it was quite wicked!'

'Was it?' said Lady de Courcy delightedly. 'But why does she lie on a sofa?'

'She has only one leg. I believe her husband beat her, and somehow her leg was injured, so she lost the use of it.'

'Unfortunate creature!' Lady de Courcy herself knew something of the difficulties of married life.

'Yes, one would pity her, if she only had better manners. But she stares so rudely! And she behaves so badly with men!'

'Oh dear!' said Lady de Courcy.

'You see that clergyman with red hair, standing near her? Through my efforts he became the bishop's chaplain, but that woman has absolutely ruined him. I shall be forced to require him to leave the palace, and he may even have to leave the Church!'

'What a fool the man must be!'

But this enjoyable conversation was interrupted by the squire, who came to take Lady de Courcy to her seat in the garden tent, and another gentleman, who was to accompany Mrs Proudie.

As the meal started, Eleanor found herself sitting between Bertie Stanhope and Mr Slope. From her seat near the entrance to the tent, she could see, through the open door of the sitting room, Mr Arabin hanging over the signora's sofa.

The garden party

Mr Arabin had passed the previous night alone in the vicar's house at St Ewold's. It was his first night there, and a dull evening it had been. Mrs Grantly had been right in saying that a priestess was needed there. He had sat there alone, with his glass in front of him, and then his teapot, thinking about Eleanor Bold. He did little but blame her – blame her for liking Mr Slope, blame her for not liking *him*, blame her for being independent and passionate. And yet the more he thought of her, the more he loved her. Then he was annoyed with her again. Why had she refused to answer a plain question, and put an end to his misery? Mr Arabin slept little that night.

When he arrived next morning at Ullathorne, he was in a state of confused uncertainty and hope, until the moment when he saw Mr Slope hand Eleanor out of her carriage. At once he assumed that she had invited him to accompany her, and that news of their engagement would follow, as night follows day. Soon afterwards he heard from Eleanor's own lips that she had come with Mr Slope; Mr Arabin's agony of suffering prevented him from understanding that she and Mr Slope had both been guests of the Stanhopes.

He wandered aimlessly into the house, avoiding conversation with anyone. And when the signora was carried in, he was feeling too weak to resist the temptation of her beauty, so, hardly knowing what he was doing, he went to sit beside her.

It is impossible to discover how she gained this knowledge, but the signora knew Mr Arabin was in love with Mrs Bold. It was therefore quite natural for her to wish to trap him, to prove to herself that her charms were greater than the widow's. She had had almost enough of Mr Slope, although it was fun to drive a very self-important chaplain to madness by a desperate and ruinous passion. But Mr Arabin was a bigger and better fly; unlike Mr Slope, he was a highly intelligent, well-educated gentleman.

'What is the matter, Mr Arabin?' she asked playfully. 'Your friend Mr Slope was here a moment ago, full of good humour. Why don't you rival him?'

Mr Arabin shuddered visibly, and Madeline knew at once he was jealous of Mr Slope. 'You and he are complete opposites,' she continued. 'He loves to be praised, you foolishly do not. He is proud and confident; he will allow nothing to stop him achieving his ambitions. You are modest and self-doubting; you are too easily persuaded to give up your dearest hopes and dreams.'

Mr Arabin was very surprised. How did this woman he hardly knew understand the secrets of his heart?

'Mr Slope is born to be successful,' Madeline went on. 'When you see him raised to a high position, with wealth, a charming wife and family, you will begin to envy him and wish you had done the same.'

'Perhaps that is true,' Mr Arabin admitted honestly.

'Remember, Mr Arabin, the good things of this world are always worth winning. That includes beautiful women. But you must fight for them! I can see Mrs Bold looking at you from the garden tent. What do you think of her as a companion for life?'

Mr Arabin glanced towards the garden and caught Eleanor looking at him. She looked quickly away. 'I am afraid Mrs Bold is engaged to another,' he said. 'She is a very beautiful, intelligent woman. It is impossible to know her without admiring her.'

'And you dare to tell me this, when you know I claim to be a beauty myself!' The signora pretended to be angry.

The garden party

'You are more beautiful, perhaps more clever. But—'
'Thank you, Mr Arabin. I knew we would be friends.'
'But Mrs Bold is the one who—'
'I won't hear another word. As long as she is in second place to me, I am happy. Now Mr Arabin, I am dying of hunger. Just fetch me a plate of food and a glass of wine, and then go to have your own lunch.'

In a sort of dream, Mr Arabin did as he was told. And as she watched him go into the garden tent, Madeline knew she had read his heart, and was amazed at his honesty. He was the first man who had not tried to court or flatter her, and whose words she felt she could trust. This endeared him to her. And as it seemed unlikely that Eleanor would agree to marry Bertie, Madeline decided to do good for once in her life, and give up Mr Arabin to the woman whom he loved. Not only that, she would do everything in her power to assist his courtship.

A declaration of love

In the garden tent, the meal was coming to an end. Mr Slope decided that it was the right time to make his declaration to the widow. He had not hesitated to drink his share of wine, in order to give himself the necessary courage. And now he followed Eleanor as she left the tent and walked quickly out into the gardens, which were almost as deserted as he could wish.

As soon as she realized she was being pursued, Eleanor turned on Mr Slope. 'Please don't let me take you from the party,' said she, with all the stiffness she knew how to use. 'I beg you, Mr Slope, to go back.'

But Mr Slope would not allow himself to be dismissed like that. He saw she was angry with him. Poor lady! She was probably unhappy that, while people had been talking of her possible marriage to him, she had been unable to announce it to the world. 'You must permit me to accompany you,' he said. 'I could not think of allowing you to walk alone.'

'Indeed you must, Mr Slope,' said Eleanor, still very stiffly. 'It is my special wish to be alone.'

Mr Slope saw that it must be now or never. 'Do not ask me to leave you, Mrs Bold,' he said with a tender yet passionate look, 'until I have spoken the words with which my heart is full.'

Eleanor now understood what she was about to go through, and the knowledge of it made her very miserable. She could refuse Mr Slope, but the fact of his making her an offer would prove the archdeacon right and herself wrong.

'I don't know what you can have to say to me, Mr Slope, that

A declaration of love

you could not say to me over lunch,' she replied, looking at him in a way that ought to have frozen him.

But gentlemen are not easily frozen when they are full of wine, and at no time would it have been easy to freeze Mr Slope. 'There are things, Mrs Bold, which a man cannot well say before a crowd,' he whispered. He repeated his tender, passionate look.

Eleanor had not wanted to stand still in front of the garden tent and receive his offer in full view of Miss Thorne's guests. So she had walked on, and Mr Slope offered her his arm.

'Thank you, Mr Slope, but for the very short time I shall remain with you, I prefer to walk alone.'

'And must it be so short?' said he, 'must it be—'

'Yes,' said Eleanor, interrupting him, 'as short as possible, if you please, sir.'

'I had hoped, Mrs Bold – I had hoped—'

'Kindly hope for nothing from me, Mr Slope. Our friendship is very slight and will probably remain that way.'

Mr Slope was still determined to be very tender, but he was also feeling rather angry. The widow seemed to have no idea of the honour she was about to receive. 'That is cruel,' said he. 'The Church allows the worst of us to hope, at least!' There was a pause. 'Beautiful woman!' he cried at last. 'Beautiful woman, you cannot pretend to be unaware that I love you! Yes, Eleanor, yes, I love you. Next to my hopes of heaven are my hopes of possessing you!' (Mr Slope's memory was faulty here, or he would have mentioned the post of dean.) 'Say, Eleanor, dearest Eleanor, shall we walk that sweet path to heaven together?'

Eleanor had no intention of ever walking together with Mr Slope on any path in future, but felt she ought to allow him to finish his speech before she answered him.

'Ah! Eleanor, will it not be sweet to travel hand in hand through the valley of life? Ah! Eleanor—'

'My name, Mr Slope, is Mrs Bold,' said Eleanor, her disgust at this familiarity overcoming her desire to be polite.

'Sweetest angel, be not so cold,' said he, and as he said it, the wine he had drunk encouraged him to put an arm round her waist, as a proof of his feelings for her.

She jumped away from him as if he were a snake, and then, quick as a flash, she raised her little hand and smacked him hard on the ear. The sound rang among the trees like a clap of thunder.

The moment she had done it, she regretted it, as an unladylike thing to do. She was tempted to beg his pardon, but fortunately thought better of it. 'I will never, never speak another word to you!' she said breathlessly, and ran quickly back along the path to the house.

Being hit by a woman was as much an insult to Mr Slope as being hit by a man. His face was sore and his pride was badly injured. He was extremely angry with the widow, and bitter thoughts of revenge filled his head. But after a while he recovered his calmness, and walked slowly back to the garden tent, taking a different direction from Eleanor. Here he heard that the dean had just died, and so he wasted no more time at Ullathorne, but returned to Barchester as speedily as possible.

As Eleanor approached the house, she saw Charlotte Stanhope and ran across the grass to join her friend.

'Oh Charlotte!' she sobbed. 'I'm glad I've found you!'

'Why, what's the matter?' said Miss Stanhope, seeing that there were tears on Eleanor's face and her hands were trembling. 'What can I do to help? Can Bertie do anything?'

'Oh no, no, no,' said Eleanor. 'Only, that hateful man—'

'What hateful man?' asked Charlotte, interested.

'Mr Slope. He's a disgusting, wicked man, and it would teach him a lesson if I told the bishop all about it!'

'Believe me, if you want to cause trouble for him, you had far better tell Mrs Proudie. But what did he do?'

'Why did he think he could court me? I never gave him any encouragement, only defended him when others criticized him.'

'That's just it, my dear. He heard about that, and therefore imagined that you were in love with him.'

Eleanor knew Charlotte was right about Mr Slope, as her family had been. She sincerely regretted her defence of him, and promised herself she would never fight against injustice again.

'But what did he do?' asked Charlotte again.

'He – he talked such dreadful nonsense about religion and heaven and love. And then – he took hold of me!'

'By the waist?'

'Yes,' said Eleanor, shuddering. 'Then I got away from him and smacked his face and ran along the path until I saw you!'

'Ha, ha, ha!' Charlotte laughed heartily at the thought of Mr Slope's embarrassment. But her aim was to endear herself to Mrs Bold, so she was quick to stop laughing and offer sympathy.

She was eager for her brother to propose and be accepted as soon as possible. Bertie's debts, and Dr Stanhope's disapproval of his son, were so great that Bertie would have to leave England at once, unless he could be sure of the widow's fortune. Luckily, it was clear that Mr Slope was no longer a rival, and now was the perfect opportunity for Bertie to make his declaration, and win the lady.

So Charlotte played what she hoped would be the final move

of the game. She persuaded Eleanor to let her arrange their departure from Ullathorne. Madeline, Charlotte, and the servants would leave first in the Stanhopes' carriage, which would then return to take Dr Stanhope, Bertie, and Eleanor home. Mr Slope would be asked to make his own way back. (He had already done this, but they were unaware of the fact.)

In order to gain the signora's approval of these arrangements, Charlotte took Eleanor into the sitting room, where they found Mr Arabin sitting beside Madeline's sofa. He got up when he saw Eleanor, and they had a short, awkward conversation while the two sisters were talking to each other.

'It has been a very pleasant party,' said Mr Arabin.

'Very,' agreed Eleanor, who had never in her life passed a more unpleasant day.

'I hope Mr Harding has enjoyed himself.'

'Oh yes, very much,' said Eleanor, who had not seen her father since soon after her arrival.

'I hope Mrs Grantly is quite well.'

'She seemed to be quite well. She is here, unless, that is, she has already left.'

'Oh yes. I was talking to her just now. Looking very well indeed.' And then Mr Arabin, finding it impossible to say any more, stood silent until Charlotte finished her conversation, and Mrs Bold stood equally silent, occupied in arranging her rings.

Finally Charlotte and Eleanor set off in search of Bertie. They found him sitting comfortably on the grass, smoking a cigarette and telling a young man he had just met about Italy.

'Bertie, I've been looking for you everywhere,' said Charlotte. 'Come here at once.'

Bertie looked up and saw them. From the first moment of

A declaration of love

meeting her, he had liked Eleanor Bold. If she had had no fortune, and he had not been obeying Charlotte's orders, he would have fallen violently in love with her. But now he regarded her, not as a beautiful woman, but as a way of making money. This new profession, called marriage, did not attract him at all.

However, he threw away his cigarette and joined the ladies, giving his arm to Eleanor. Charlotte told him the whole story of Mr Slope's misbehaviour, and put Eleanor under her brother's protection. She then hurried away, leaving Bertie to walk with the widow alone.

Bertie Stanhope was idle, but he was not wicked. He was beginning to feel that this plan of Charlotte's, which involved his catching Mrs Bold and living on her money instead of his father's, was too deliberate and cold-blooded for him. And indeed, if he were successful with Eleanor, what would be his reward? A quiet life in Barchester by the widow's fireside; his highest excitement would be the occasional dinner at Plumstead, if, of course, the archdeacon ever agreed to receive him there. He wondered if he could find a way of obeying Charlotte and at the same time saving the widow from marriage to him.

'Mrs Bold,' he began very seriously, 'I may have to leave Barchester. I must take up a profession of some kind.'

'I think you *could* take an interest in some sort of work, Mr Stanhope,' said Eleanor, who felt a friendly fondness for him.

'In this matter I am determined to be guided completely by you.' And Bertie turned to face her on the path. In their walk they had come to the exact place where Eleanor had raised her hand to Mr Slope's face. Was she to receive another proposal here, so soon after the chaplain's? 'We have been very good friends, Mrs Bold, have we not?' Bertie continued.

'Yes, I think we have.'

'Please don't be angry with me, Mrs Bold. I must confess it all to you. My dear sister Charlotte only thinks of my happiness, and – wants me to marry you!'

'Mrs Bold, I may have to leave Barchester,' said Bertie.

A declaration of love

Suddenly Eleanor realized why Charlotte had always been so charming and hospitable towards her – it had all been a plan to get hold of her income for Bertie's benefit! She was horrified.

'I must tell you,' continued Bertie in embarrassment, 'that my sister's hopes for me are higher than my own.'

'But if you do not yourself wish to marry me, then why are you telling me this?' asked Eleanor, angry at such an insulting pretence of a proposal.

'Because I must not anger her. And, as I understand, there is no chance of my persuading you to marry me, I would very much like you to tell her that I did propose to you, but that you simply turned me down.'

This was beyond everything! Eleanor was furious, and deeply offended; she certainly would not lie, to prevent his sister being angry with him. 'I regret to say it, Mr Stanhope, but after what has passed, I believe that all communication between your family and myself had better come to an end at once.'

But now her self-control broke down, and she started sobbing passionately. 'How *could* you? I thought you were a friend! Oh, I wish I were at home!'

Poor Bertie was greatly moved. 'Don't worry, I shall not annoy you any more. I'll take you to the carriage immediately. You shall share it with my father, and I'll walk home or somewhere – it doesn't much matter what I do.'

He gently handed her a handkerchief to dry her tears, and accompanied her to the house. After she had said goodbye to the Thornes, he helped her into the waiting carriage. Eleanor, looking out of the window as the carriage drove off, saw him with his hat in his hand, bowing with his usual cheerful smile. It was many a long year before she saw him again.

10
A woman's friendship

Before setting off for the garden party at Ullathorne, Mrs Proudie had spoken to her lord, once and for all, about the post of warden. She was determined that Mr Quiverful should have it.

'Bishop,' she had said to him immediately after breakfast, 'have you signed the appointment yet?'

'No, my dear, it is not exactly signed yet.'

'Then do it,' said the lady.

The bishop did it. Mrs Proudie herself wrote to Mr and Mrs Quiverful, asking them to come to the palace at eleven o'clock the next morning. Then the Proudies drove to Ullathorne, where the bishop spent a very pleasant day. And in the evening he was given a glass of wine in his wife's sitting room, and allowed to read his newspaper comfortably by the fire. What great comfort there is for husbands who obey their wives!

Mr and Mrs Quiverful's hopes were raised again when they received Mrs Proudie's letter, but this time they were not disappointed. When they presented themselves at the bishop's palace as requested, they were told the good news at once. That evening there was great joy at Puddingdale, with so much kissing and crying and laughing that they almost forgot to eat.

On that same day Mr Slope was delighted to find that his journalist friend, Mr Towers, had written a most flattering article about him in *The Jupiter*. It said:

'It is now five years since we called our readers' attention to Hiram's Hospital in the quiet city of Barchester. There is now another matter in Barchester that we wish to comment on. Dr Trefoil, the dean, died yesterday. His only fault was his great age, which is something we all hope to be guilty of. But we consider that this post should now be filled by a much younger man, who has the energy and strength to work for the good of the Church. Mr Obadiah Slope's name has been mentioned to us. He is at present the bishop's chaplain. A better man could hardly be found. He is young, enthusiastic, knowledgeable and, we believe, a truly good man. Such a choice would go far to raise public confidence in the present system of Church appointments, and would show people that, from now on, our Church will not offer easy, well-paid work to elderly, worn-out clergymen.'

Mr Slope read this article with considerable satisfaction. Sixty thousand copies of *The Jupiter*, distributed around the country, were, in his eyes, the most powerful way of influencing public opinion. He was very grateful to Mr Towers, and looked forward to the day when he, as dean, would entertain his friend to an excellent dinner.

But his feelings were not all of triumph. He was still angry with the widow, for the way in which she had refused his proposal. And he would have liked to hate the signora, but he was passionately attracted to her and could not resist her charms.

Poor Mrs Bold was very unhappy when she got home from Ullathorne, and also quite exhausted. She found her sister-in-law, Mary, in the sitting room, playing with little Johnny.

'Oh Mary, I'm so glad you didn't go!' cried Eleanor. 'It was an awful party!'

'I have nothing to regret, then,' said Mary cheerfully.

'*You* have nothing to regret, but oh! Mary, I have – so much!'

and Eleanor began wildly kissing her boy, while tears ran down her face.

'Good heavens, Eleanor, what is the matter?' asked Mary, concerned. 'Let me make you some tea. You are tired.'

At first Eleanor was unwilling to tell Mary what had happened, because Mary had never approved of the friendship with Mr Slope. But Mary was so kind and so comforting that Eleanor soon told her the whole story, and felt much better for it. There was not the slightest touch of triumph about Mary; she never said, 'I told you so,' but sympathized strongly with Eleanor.

'I know I was wrong,' said Eleanor, 'to hit Mr Slope, but I had to protect myself.'

'He certainly deserved it!' said Mary firmly.

'If I'd stabbed him with a knife, he would have deserved it! But what will they say about it at Plumstead?'

'I don't think I would tell them, if I were you,' said Mary. And Eleanor began to think she would not.

The next day Eleanor stayed at home, but she heard the news that the dean had died, and that Mr Quiverful had been appointed warden. In the evening her father came to visit her, and she had to repeat the story, or as much of it as she could bring herself to tell him. He did not seem surprised at Mr Slope's declaration of love. So she asked him if he had expected it.

'I do not think it at all strange that anyone should admire my Eleanor,' he replied fondly.

'But I did not give him the slightest encouragement!'

Mr Harding thought it safer not to reply to this, but simply said, 'You'll tell the archdeacon? Or Susan? You'll tell them they were wrong about you wanting to marry that man?'

'I shall never willingly mention Mr Slope's name to either of them,' said Eleanor, a little stiffly. 'But father, is it true you are not going to be warden, after all?'

'Yes, my dear, quite true. And I am delighted for Mr Quiverful and his large family. I am getting old now, and my main wish is for peace and quiet, not for constant arguments with the bishop, his chaplain, and the archdeacon. I shall never starve, you know,' he added laughing, 'as long as you are here.'

'But will you come and live with me here, father? It would make me so very happy if you did!'

'No, thank you, my dear, I'm quite satisfied with my rooms in the High Street. But I *will* have dinner with you tonight!'

Later that evening, Eleanor and Mary were singing while he was playing the piano, when a maid entered the room. She brought a very small note in a beautiful pink envelope; it quite filled the room with perfume as it lay on the silver dish.

'The servant is waiting for an answer, madam,' said the maid.

Eleanor blushed as she took the note. She guessed it came from the signora. The note said:

Thursday evening

My dear Mrs Bold,

May I ask you, if you would be so kind, to call on me tomorrow. Please say what time would best suit you. I need hardly say that if I could call on you, I would not ask you to come to me. I partly know what happened the other day, and I promise that you shall meet with no annoyance if you come. My brother leaves us for London today, and from there he goes to Italy. I have something of considerable importance to say to you. Please excuse me, therefore, for writing to you, even if you do not agree to my request.

Believe me, I am, very sincerely, yours,
    Madeline Neroni

The three of them read this letter together, and decided, after some discussion, that Eleanor should send a reply, saying she would see the signora at twelve o'clock the next day.

When Charlotte had arrived home from the Ullathorne party the previous day, she had waited eagerly for the carriage to return with Bertie, and, she hoped, the news of his engagement to Mrs Bold. But it was only her father's step that she heard in the hall, and she realized her brother's attempt at courting the widow must have failed. This was disappointing, but not completely unexpected.

She was called to her father's room, and when she entered, found him angrier than she had ever seen him before.

'Tell me where your brother is, and what his plans for the future are now!' ordered the old man. 'I'm glad that charming Mrs Bold is not going to be sacrificed to such an idle, heartless young man as my son! Marriage, indeed! Who would marry *him*? It was just a foolish idea of yours!'

'Father, it's no use scolding me. I've done my best for him and you.'

Her father sighed deeply. 'He'll ruin me, with his debts! I've made up my mind, Charlotte. He shall eat and drink no more in this house! He must leave. I don't care where he goes.'

'Very well. Then I suppose he must go back to Italy. Life is cheaper there.' And Charlotte, by using all her powers of persuasion, managed to get her father to agree to make his son one last payment, as long as Bertie left England the next day.

Dr Stanhope was angry with Madeline too, for expecting him to pay all her bills, and for behaving so badly with all the unmarried men in Barchester. He was even angry with Charlotte,

A woman's friendship

for defending her brother and sister. He felt that his children had damaged his reputation in the city, and Charlotte realized that the whole family, not just Bertie, would have to return to Italy soon.

But two days later, when Eleanor arrived at the Stanhopes' house, Bertie had already left for Italy, and the house was peaceful. She was shown up to the signora's private sitting room, without seeing any of the family, which was a great relief to her.

'This is very kind of you, Mrs Bold, very kind, after what has happened,' said the signora, with her sweetest smile.

'Your letter almost obliged me to come.'

'That is true. But how cold you are to me! I know you have good reason to be displeased with us all. But I did not send for you to talk about that. Please come closer to me, Mrs Bold.'

Eleanor obeyed, bringing her chair closer to the sofa.

'And now I am going to tell you something, Mrs Bold, which you may think is too personal. But I know I am right to do so. I believe you know Mr Arabin?'

Eleanor would have given the world not to blush, but her blood was not at her own command. She did blush, right up to her hair, and the signora, who had asked her to come closer in order to observe her face, saw it.

'If you know Mr Arabin, I'm sure you must like him,' continued Madeline. 'Everyone who knows him must like him.'

Mrs Bold could not speak. She felt hot and faint.

'How stiff you are with me,' said Madeline. 'And yet I'm doing for you all that one woman can do to serve another.'

The widow began to think that perhaps the signora's friendship was real. Then another thought came to her – Mr Arabin was too precious to lose. Even if she felt scorn for the signora and her way of life, perhaps Madeline could help her.

'I don't want to be stiff,' she said, trying to excuse herself, 'but this conversation is so very strange!'

'Well, then, it may become stranger still,' said Madeline, turning her own face full on her companion's. 'Do you love him, love him with all your heart and soul? Because I can tell you, he loves you, thinks of you and nothing else, is thinking of you now as he attempts to write his sermon for next Sunday's service. What would I not give to be loved in such a way by such a man!'

Mrs Bold stood up, speechless, and took the signora's hand. Madeline went on, 'What I tell you is God's own truth, and it is for you to use it for your own happiness. But you must not betray me. You know his secret now, and I advise you to use the knowledge. And remember, he is not like other men. You mustn't expect him to come to you with pretty presents, to kneel at your feet and to flatter you. There are plenty of men who do that, but he is not one of them. With him, yes means yes, and no means no. Even if his heart should break, the woman who refuses him once will have refused him for ever. And now, Mrs Bold, I will not keep you. If ever you are a happy wife in that man's house, I and my family will be far away. But I shall expect you to write me one line to say you have forgiven the sins of the Stanhope family.'

Eleanor half whispered that she would, and then crept out of the room, down the stairs and out into the open air. The fact that this woman, whom she could never like, knew so much about her and the man she loved, was damaging to her pride. But soon this feeling was swept away in the wild joy that filled her heart – he loved her! She was fully determined to follow Madeline's advice; if he ever proposed to her, her 'yes' would certainly be 'yes'.

A woman's friendship

On the following day the signora was in her brightest morning dress, and had a whole group of men around her sofa. The first to come and the last to leave was Mr Arabin, to whom the signora was unusually kind and gentle. Mr Thorne was there too, in his best suit; even a respectable, fifty-year-old gentleman could fall into the signora's trap. There were also a number of eager young clergymen, smaller flies who could not keep away from such a powerful, beautiful spider.

And then came Mr Slope. All the world knew that he was generally considered likely to become dean. He therefore held his head high and walked in a self-important way, as a dean might.

The signora had been looking forward to his visit. 'Mr Slope,' said she, 'I hear you are triumphing on all sides.'

'What do you mean?' he asked, smiling. He did not dislike people connecting his name with the post of dean.

'You are the winner, both in love and war,' she replied.

Mr Slope did not look quite so satisfied now.

'Mr Arabin,' she continued, 'don't you think Mr Slope is a very lucky man?'

'Not more than he deserves, I'm sure,' said Mr Arabin.

'He is to be our new dean, you know, Mr Thorne,' she said to the squire, who was trying to follow the conversation.

'Really, signora?' asked Mr Thorne doubtfully.

'Yes, indeed. And not only that, he is to have a wife too. A wife with a large fortune. When will it be, Mr Slope?'

'When will what be?' said Mr Slope, pretending to smile.

'Your marriage, Mr Slope. Now do tell us, we're all dying to know, when is the widow to be made Mrs Dean?'

To Mr Arabin this conversation was peculiarly painful, but he could not stop listening.

'Come, come, Mr Slope,' continued the signora. 'We all know you proposed to her the other day at Ullathorne. How did she accept you? With a simple "yes", or with the two "no's" which make a "yes"? Or some other way? Tell us, do!'

Mr Slope had never in his life felt so embarrassed. Everybody in the room was looking at him, ready to laugh at his discomfort, except for Mr Arabin, who was staring miserably at him. This was the moment to think of a sharp reply to the signora, but nothing came to mind; he had not a word to say.

'It's good to be off with the old love, Before you are on with the new!' sang the signora.

The signora had no pity; she knew nothing of mercy, now that she had Mr Slope in her power. 'No answer, Mr Slope? It can't possibly be that the woman was fool enough to refuse you! Perhaps she wasn't satisfied with a dean, but is waiting for a bishop to come along! Now here is a piece of advice for you, Mr Slope. Listen carefully,' and she started singing,

It's good to be happy and wise, *Mr Slope,*
It's good to be honest and true,
It's good to be off with the old love, *Mr Slope,*
Before you are on with the new!

'Ha, ha, ha!' And the signora, throwing herself back on her sofa, laughed heartily. She had taken her revenge on him, for courting herself and Mrs Bold at the same time.

How Mr Slope got out of that room, he never knew. Possibly he was given some assistance. But when he reached the fresh air of the street, he realized that at last his love for the signora was cured. Whenever he thought of her in his dreams from now on, she did not appear as a beautiful angel, but as a hateful devil.

11
The new dean

At Plumstead, the archdeacon was in a state of misery. Not only had Mr Quiverful, rather than Mr Harding, been appointed warden of Hiram's Hospital, it also seemed quite possible that Mr Slope would become dean, and marry Eleanor Bold. There was yet another reason for anxiety. Dr Grantly's excellent and respected friend, Francis Arabin, of whose qualities he had boasted so loudly, was misbehaving himself. People were now beginning to talk of his repeated visits to the signora. This was not at all what was expected of the vicar of St Ewold's.

Just as the archdeacon and his wife were discussing these matters, they heard a carriage drive up to the door at high speed.

'Whoever can it be, Susan?' said Dr Grantly, as he opened the sitting room door into the hall. 'Why, it's your father!'

It was indeed Mr Harding, bursting to tell his news.

'We're very glad to see you, father,' said his daughter. 'I'll go and get your room ready at once.'

'Don't go just yet, Susan,' said Mr Harding. 'I have something to tell you. Or shall I wait till after dinner?'

'If you have anything important to tell us,' said the archdeacon, 'I beg you, let us hear it at once. Has Eleanor gone off with Slope?'

'No, she has not,' said Mr Harding, looking displeased.

'Has Slope been made dean?'

'No, he has not, but—'

'But what?' said the archdeacon impatiently.

'They have offered it to me,' said Mr Harding modestly.

The new dean

'Good heavens!' cried the archdeacon.

'My dear, dear father!' cried Mrs Grantly and threw her arms round her father's neck.

And after they had both congratulated Mr Harding, they all sat down to dinner. The archdeacon's joy was uncontrollable. It was not until they had finished eating and the servants had left, that Mr Harding found the opportunity to say, rather nervously, 'It's very kind of the prime minister, and I'm most grateful for the offer, but I'm afraid I can't accept it.'

The archdeacon was so shocked that he almost dropped his glass. Why would a vicar earning less than £200 a year not wish to gain one of the most desirable positions in the Church, at an income of £1200? But Mr Harding explained to him and Susan, over and over again, that he would be incapable of doing the job properly, and that at his age he did not want any sort of promotion. In spite of their protests, he remained firm.

This was another disappointment for the archdeacon. Nothing would have suited him better than to have his father-in-law as dean, but it was impossible to change Mr Harding's mind.

At Ullathorne, the squire's sister had also heard the stories about Mr Arabin and the signora. Miss Thorne was of the opinion that all vicars should be married, in order to avoid this kind of unpleasantness, and with her usual good-hearted energy she set to work to find a wife for Mr Arabin. In looking through the list of her unmarried friends who might possibly want a husband, and who had the right qualities to be a vicar's wife, she could think of no one more suitable than Mrs Bold. So, losing no time, she invited Mrs Bold and her small son to come and stay for a month or two at Ullathorne. 'We'll have Mr Arabin too,' said

Miss Thorne to herself, 'and in twelve or eighteen months' time, if all goes well, Mrs Bold will take up residence at St Ewold's.' And the kind-hearted lady praised herself for her matchmaking.

Eleanor was a little surprised at the invitation, but accepted it, and arrived at Ullathorne the day before her father was offered the post of dean. Since her interview with Madeline, she had done little else but think about Mr Arabin, and she was hoping to see him at Ullathorne. If only they could meet, and speak to each other!

And they did meet there. Mr Arabin, Eleanor discovered, was also staying with the Thornes. He arrived during the morning and found the two ladies sewing in the sitting room. Miss Thorne had no idea that her immediate absence would be a blessing, and remained talking to her guests until lunch-time. After lunch Mr Arabin returned to his church duties, and Eleanor and Miss Thorne took a walk together.

When they returned, Eleanor was left alone in the sitting room, and just as it was getting dark, Mr Arabin came in. It was a beautiful autumn afternoon, and Eleanor was sitting near the window to get the last of the daylight for her reading. Mr Arabin stood with his back to the fire and his hands in his pockets, making a few ordinary remarks about the weather.

'The sky does look lovely,' said Eleanor.

He could not see the sky from where he was standing, so he had to go close to her. 'Very lovely,' said he, modestly keeping at a distance to avoid touching her dress. Then he seemed to have nothing further to say, so he returned to the fire.

Eleanor could not think what to say, and, moreover, found she could not prevent herself from crying. She hoped he would not notice. He was not looking at her, so it did not seem likely.

The new dean

'Do you like Ullathorne?' he asked, from his safely distant position. 'I don't mean Mr and Miss Thorne, I mean the house. There is something about old-fashioned houses and gardens that especially pleases me.'

'I like everything old-fashioned,' said Eleanor. 'Old-fashioned things are so much more honest.'

'I hardly know whether to agree with you or not.'

'I think the world grows more ambitious and selfish every day,' said Eleanor.

'That is because you see more of it than when you were younger. But we should not judge by what we see – we see so very, very little.' There was an uncomfortable pause while Mr Arabin turned over the coins in his pockets. Then he started walking uneasily up and down the room.

Eleanor sat silently with her face bent over her book. She was afraid her tears would overcome her, and was preparing to escape from the room, when suddenly Mr Arabin stopped walking and turned to face her.

'Mrs Bold,' said he, 'I owe you a humble apology for asking you that extremely personal question, about – about a certain gentleman. I had no right to do it.'

Eleanor was most anxious to say something polite and encouraging, but did not want to betray her feelings.

'Indeed, I was not offended, Mr Arabin.'

'Oh, but you were! Quite rightly! I have not forgiven myself, but I hope to hear that you forgive me.'

She could no longer speak calmly, although she still continued to hide her tears. Mr Arabin, after waiting a moment for her reply, was walking towards the door. Rising from her seat, she gently touched his arm and said, 'Oh, Mr Arabin, do not go till

I speak to you! I do forgive you. You know that I forgive you.'

He took her hand, and then looked into her face, to read his whole future there, as if written in a book. The eagerness and sadness of his expression moved Eleanor so much that she could not look back at him. She dropped her eyes to the ground, let her tears roll unchecked down her face, and left her hand within his.

It was only for a minute that they stood like that, but it was a minute that they would remember for ever. Eleanor was sure now that she was loved. But why did he not speak to her? Could it be that he looked to her to make the first sign? And he, although he knew very little of women, even he knew that he was loved. He had only to ask, and it would all be his own, this inexpressible loveliness, this bright and loving nature which had so attracted him from the first. She must love him! Otherwise she would never allow her hand to remain so long within his own. He had only to ask. Ah, but that was the difficulty!

'Mrs Bold . . .' he said at last, and stopped. 'Eleanor!' he then said, very softly, still lacking a lover's courage, and fearful of giving offence. She looked gently up into his face. 'Eleanor!' he said again, and in a moment he had her in his arms. How this happened, neither of them knew, but there was now a sympathy between them that hardly allowed them to be individuals – they were one and the same – one body, one soul, one life.

'Eleanor, my own Eleanor, my own, my wife!' As she shyly looked up at him through her tears, he pressed his lips to her forehead. For the first time in his life, he kissed a woman.

'Oh, let me go now,' said she. 'I am too happy to remain – I must be alone.' He let her go, and she rushed out of the room.

Once in the privacy of her bedroom, she was able to sob and cry and laugh, as the hopes and fears and miseries of the last few

The new dean

weeks passed through her mind. What happiness she could now look forward to!

After dinner that evening she told Miss Thorne, in a voice trembling with joy, that she was engaged to Mr Arabin.

Poor Miss Thorne was a little shocked at the speed with which her plan had succeeded. They were not young lovers, but a forty-year-old vicar and a respectable widow, and only a day had been long enough for them to arrange matters, where Miss Thorne had allowed twelve to eighteen months! She was almost disappointed, and, shaking her head regretfully, thought it must be the modern way of doing things. But on the whole she was pleased that her matchmaking had been so successful, and wished Eleanor much happiness.

The next morning Eleanor returned to Barchester, and very soon received a visit from her father. How much each of them had to tell the other! Mr Harding told his daughter about being invited to become dean, and Eleanor told her father about her engagement to Francis Arabin. Mr Harding was quite delighted to hear who his new son-in-law was to be, and was happy to spend most of the morning discussing Mr Arabin's good qualities with Eleanor. However, he refused to say any more about the post of dean, because a new idea had entered his head – why should Mr Arabin not be the new dean?

They were still talking when Eleanor saw the archdeacon's carriage through the window.

'Oh my dear,' said her father, 'Dr Grantly said he would come and see you, but I forgot to mention it.'

Eleanor could not, in the first hours of her joy, bring herself to hear the archdeacon's lengthy apologies and congratulations, so she hurried out.

The archdeacon, therefore, found Mr Harding alone when he entered the room.

'Is anything the matter with Eleanor?' asked Dr Grantly, thinking that perhaps the truth about Mr Slope had come out.

'Well, *something* is the matter. I wonder if you will be surprised at it. What do you think Mr Arabin has just done?'

'Nothing to do with that daughter of Stanhope's, surely?'

'No, not that woman,' said Mr Harding, enjoying his little joke and trying not to smile.

'Not that woman! Is he going to do anything about any woman? Why can't you speak out if you have anything to say? There's nothing I hate so much as mysteries.'

'This must remain confidential at present, archdeacon. You can tell Susan, but no one else.'

'Nonsense!' cried the archdeacon angrily. 'You can't have any secret about Arabin that I don't know!'

'Only this – he and Eleanor are engaged.'

'Arabin! It's impossible! She must be mistaken!'

It took quite a long speech from Mr Harding to convince Dr Grantly that it was not only possible, but true. At first the archdeacon was simply amazed. Then he was disgusted at his own misjudgement of the situation. But finally he began to smile, and expressed great satisfaction with the news. 'Well, well!' said he. 'Good heavens, good heavens!'

And then slowly, gradually and cleverly Mr Harding proposed his own new plan. Why should Mr Arabin not be the new dean? Slowly, gradually and thoughtfully Dr Grantly was persuaded to accept the idea. It would be the perfect solution to their difficulties with the bishop, and, with Arabin as dean, the archdeacon's influence in Barchester would be far greater.

The new dean

So it was arranged between them that they would travel to London together the following morning, to try to persuade the prime minister to appoint Mr Arabin, instead of Mr Harding.

Mr Slope was in his room at the bishop's palace, when he received a note from his friend Sir Nicholas, informing him that he would not be offered the post of dean. He did not give way to despair, however, but sat down quietly to make a new plan for his future. He counted up his money, and then he wrote a letter to a rich factory-owner's wife in London, who, as he well knew, had entertained and encouraged serious young clergymen in the past.

A few moments later a servant appeared, to ask him to go to the bishop's study at once. Mr Slope waited ten minutes to prove his independence, and then went to the bishop's room. As he had expected, Mrs Proudie was there with her husband.

'Mr Slope,' said the bishop, 'I must speak to you about an urgent matter, concerning yourself.'

'My lord, if I may express a wish, I would prefer no discussion to take place in the presence of a third person.'

'Don't alarm yourself, Mr Slope,' said the lady. 'No discussion is at all necessary. The bishop will only express his own wishes, that is all.'

'I will only express my own wishes, that is all,' the bishop repeated. 'No discussion is at all necessary.'

'May I ask if I have done anything wrong, my lord?' enquired Mr Slope, looking innocent.

'Do you dare to ask the bishop that?' cried Mrs Proudie.

'Mrs Proudie, I will not have words with you.'

'Ah sir, but you will have words! Why have you had so many words with that Signora Neroni? Disgraceful behaviour! You are no longer wanted by the bishop, sir. Kindly leave his employment and this house as soon as possible!'

'My lord,' said Mr Slope, turning his back completely on the lady, 'may I have from your own lips any decision you have come to on this matter?'

'Certainly, Slope, certainly. Well, you hear what Mrs Proudie says. That is the decision I have come to on the matter.'

'If you wish to remain in Barchester,' added Mrs Proudie, 'and will promise never to see that woman again, the bishop will mention your name to Mr Quiverful, who now needs an assistant at Puddingdale. There is an income of £50 a year, I believe.'

'God forgive you, madam, for the way in which you have treated me,' said Mr Slope. 'As to the bishop, I pity him.' And he left the room to pack his bags, leaving Mrs Proudie victorious.

It is well known, however, that the Slopes of this world fall on their feet like cats. On his return to London he discovered that the factory-owner had died, and the widow needed comforting. Mr Slope was able to comfort her, and soon found himself living in her pleasantly large house, with her fortune at his command.

By using every influential contact they had, Dr Grantly and Mr Harding managed to persuade the prime minister's advisers that Francis Arabin should be dean. It was a happy moment for them both when, on their return to Barchester, they were able to present the prime minister's letter to their friend, appointing him Dean of Barchester. How grateful Eleanor was to her father, for giving up his chance of promotion to his future son-in-law!

A few months later, Mr Arabin married Mrs Bold. The wedding dress, the carriages, the flowers, the reception – everything was paid for by the archdeacon, who could not do enough to show

The new dean

how sorry he was to have doubted Eleanor, and how happy he was to have triumphed over Slope.

Now Eleanor and her husband live in the dean's house in perfect happiness. Mr Harding has gone to live with them there, and spends much of his time teaching little Johnny to sing and play the piano. Another child is expected soon, and Susan Grantly is looking forward to helping her sister with the new baby. Now that Eleanor is also a clergyman's wife, she and Susan get on much better than in the past.

The Stanhopes are living in Italy again. Not long after their return there, the signora received a pretty, but short letter from Mrs Arabin. This was answered by a bright, charming and amusing note, as the signora's letters always were. Here ended the friendship between Eleanor and the Stanhopes.

Dr Proudie is still bishop, but has never attempted to disobey his wife again. He prefers being henpecked to having an uncomfortable domestic life. And Mrs Proudie, now that she is certain of her power, interferes hardly at all in spiritual matters. Dr Grantly and Mr Arabin, whose views on religion are so similar, work together on all church business. So priestly arguments are a thing of the past, now that war is over, and peace has returned to that ancient cathedral city of Barchester.

GLOSSARY

agony extreme mental pain

angel (here) a person who is very good and kind

archbishop a bishop of the highest rank, responsible for all the churches in a large area

archdeacon a priest just below the rank of bishop

bishop a senior priest in charge of the work of the Church in a city or district

bless to ask God to protect someone or something; **blessing** *(n)*

blush *(v)* to become red in the face because you are embarrassed or ashamed

cathedral the main church of a district, under the care of a bishop

chaplain a priest who works as an assistant to a bishop

Church of England the official Church in England, sometimes called the Anglican Church

Church of Rome the Roman Catholic Church

clergyman a male priest in the Christian Church; **clergy** *(plural)*

court *(old-fashioned)* to try (for a man) to make a woman love you and want to marry you; **courtship** *(n)*

cripple *(old-fashioned)* a person who is unable to walk because of injury

dean a priest of high rank who is in charge of the other priests in a cathedral

debate *(v)* to discuss something, with formal speeches

disgraceful very bad or unacceptable

father-in-law the father of your husband or wife

flatter to say nice things about somebody, often in a way that is not sincere, because you want something from them

Glossary

gentleman a man who has excellent manners and always behaves well

Good heavens! an exclamation of surprise

guano the waste substance from birds that live near the sea, used to make plants and crops grow well

half-crown an old British coin worth $2\frac{1}{2}$ shillings (worth $12\frac{1}{2}$p in today's money)

henpecked a henpecked man has a wife who is always telling him what to do, and is too weak to disagree with her

honour *(n)* respect and admiration; knowing what is right and what is wrong; something you are very proud to do

honourable *(adj)* deserving respect and admiration; showing high moral standards

humble showing you realize that you make mistakes

idleness laziness; wanting to avoid hard work

liberal wanting a lot of political and economic freedom and supporting gradual social, political, or religious change

lordship (his lordship, my lord) titles of respect used when speaking about or to a bishop

maid a female servant in a house

matchmaking bringing people together in the hope that they will want to marry each other

ordain to make somebody officially a priest

priestess a female priest

prime minister the leader of the government in Britain

scorn *(n)* a strong feeling that someone is not good enough, usually shown by the way you speak

seal *(v)* to close an envelope by sticking the edges of the opening together

sermon a talk on a moral or religious subject, usually given by a priest during a service

Glossary

service a religious ceremony, often in a church

shudder to shake because you have a strong feeling of dislike or disgust

signora the Italian word for Mrs; also a polite way of speaking about a lady

sin an offence against God or against a moral or religious law

sister-in-law (here) the sister of your husband or wife

slave a person who is strongly influenced by someone or is in their power

sob *(v)* to cry noisily, taking sudden, sharp breaths

son-in-law your daughter's husband

spider a small creature with eight thin legs

squire *(old-fashioned)* a man of high social status who owns most of the land in a country area

steward a person employed to manage a large house and land

Sunday school a class organized by a church, where children can go for a short time on Sundays to learn about the Christian religion

telegraph a method of sending messages over long distances, using wires that carry electric signals

tender kind, gentle, and loving

triumph *(n)* a great success, achievement or victory

triumphant *(adj)* showing great satisfaction in victory

vicar an Anglican priest who is in charge of a church

warden (here) the person in charge of a home for old men; **wardenship** the post of warden

widow's cap a type of hat worn by a woman whose husband is dead and who has not remarried

ACTIVITIES

Before Reading

1 **Read the introduction on the first page of the book, and the back cover. What do you know now about *Barchester Towers*? For each sentence, circle Y (Yes) or N (No).**

   1 The story is about a war between different nations. Y / N
   2 Barchester is a city with a cathedral and a bishop. Y / N
   3 The new bishop is appointed by his fellow clergymen. Y / N
   4 The bishop's wife demands obedience from everyone. Y / N
   5 Mr Slope's only ambition is to help the bishop. Y / N
   6 Signora Neroni is shy in the company of men. Y / N

2 **What might these characters do in the story? Look at these ideas, and discuss which ones you think are more likely than others.**

   1 Mrs Proudie will . . .
      a) help Parson Quiverful.
      b) gain more power over her husband.
      c) run away with Mr Slope.
   2 Mr Slope will . . .
      a) become Bishop of Barchester.
      b) fall in love with Madeline Neroni.
      c) find a way of becoming a rich man.
   3 Eleanor Bold will . . .
      a) marry again.
      b) become a friend of Dr Proudie.
      c) lose her money to Mr Slope.

ACTIVITIES

While Reading

Read Chapters 1 to 3. Complete the sentences with the right characters. Which names, titles, and relationships from the lists below will fit each gap? Add *his, her, the, 's* where necessary.

- *Dr Proudie, Mrs Proudie, Mr Slope, Mr Harding, Eleanor Bold, Johnny Bold, Mary Bold, Dr Stanhope, Bertie Stanhope, Charlotte Stanhope, Madeline Neroni, Dr Grantly, Mr Quiverful*
- *archdeacon, bishop, chaplain, warden, vicar of Puddingdale*
- *wife, daughter, father, father-in-law, sister, sister-in-law, son*

1 _____ hoped to become _____ , so he asked _____ to send a message to the prime minister.
2 _____ needed help in caring for _____ , so _____ had come to live with her.
3 _____ worked for _____ as his chaplain, but shared the same strong passion for power as _____ .
4 When _____ gave his first sermon in the cathedral, there were strong reactions: _____ was furious, _____ was miserable about the music, and _____ himself was terrified by what _____ said.
5 _____ brought his family back from Italy, including _____ , who made all the young men fall in love with her.
6 _____ cleverly encouraged _____ to refuse the post of _____ , so that it could be offered to _____ .
7 _____ agreed to the plan, suggested by _____ , of marrying _____ for her thousand pounds a year.

110

ACTIVITIES: *While Reading*

Before you read Chapter 4, can you guess what might happen? Circle Y (Yes) or N (No) for each of these ideas.

1 Eleanor tells her sister about her feelings for Mr Slope. Y/ N
2 Eleanor's friendship with Bertie turns into love. Y/ N
3 The bishop makes Mr Harding the warden. Y/ N
4 Mr Slope goes directly against Mrs Proudie's wishes. Y/ N

Read Chapters 4 to 6. Who said these words, and to whom? How do these words influence your own opinion of these characters?

1 'Every church should have its priestess as well as its priest.'
2 'I have never met so much suffering, joined to such perfect beauty and such a clever mind.'
3 'I must wait for another post, that's all.'
4 'His lordship has given his word.'
5 'Mr Slope and I are very busy.'
6 'Whatever you do, never mix love and business.'
7 'My heart is all your own!'
8 'I was deceived; I believed you thought well of me.'

Before you read Chapter 7 (*Victory for Mrs Proudie*), what do you think the victory is, and how does Mrs Proudie achieve it? Choose from these ideas.

1 The victory is . . .
   a) preventing the bishop's visit to the archbishop.
   b) regaining complete control over the bishop's actions.
2 She achieves her victory over the bishop by . . .
   a) being so nice to him that he sees how pleasant life could be if he obeyed her.
   b) being so fierce that she terrifies him into obeying her.

ACTIVITIES: *While Reading*

Read Chapters 7 to 9. At the Ullathorne garden party, several people behaved badly or foolishly. Complete the sentences in your own words, saying what you think they should or should not have done.

1 When Mr Arabin saw Mr Slope hand Eleanor out of the Stanhopes' carriage, he . . .
2 When Eleanor made it very clear she wanted to be alone, Mr Slope . . .
3 When Mr Slope put his arm round Eleanor's waist, she . . .
4 When Charlotte heard from Eleanor about Mr Slope's proposal, she . . .
5 While Charlotte was talking to Madeline about the arrangements for going home, Mr Arabin . . .
6 If Bertie did not really want to marry Eleanor, he . . .
7 When Bertie told Eleanor about Charlotte's plan, he . . .

Before you read Chapter 10 (*A woman's friendship*) and Chapter 11 (*The new dean*), how do you think the story will end? Circle Y (Yes) or N (No) for each sentence.

1 Mr Quiverful becomes the warden of Hiram's Hospital. Y / N
2 Mr Slope becomes the new dean. Y / N
3 Eleanor receives some useful advice from Madeline. Y / N
4 Bertie goes back to Italy. Y / N
5 Madeline finds a second husband. Y / N
6 Miss Thorne does some matchmaking. Y / N
7 Mr Arabin marries the woman he loves. Y / N
8 Dr Proudie and Dr Grantly become good friends. Y / N

ACTIVITIES

After Reading

1 Which of these adjectives can be used to describe the characters below? Choose one or two adjectives from the list that best suit each character, in your opinion. Explain why you think the adjectives you have chosen are appropriate.

brave, cowardly, cruel, deceitful, dutiful, good-hearted, henpecked, humble, idle, impatient, interfering, loyal, oily, practical, selfish, sincere, truthful, warlike

Dr Proudie	Mr Harding	Madeline Neroni
Mrs Proudie	Eleanor Bold	Charlotte Stanhope
Mr Slope	Mr Arabin	Bertie Stanhope
Dr Grantly	Mr Quiverful	
Mrs Grantly	Mrs Quiverful	

2 Eleanor wrote a 'pretty, but short letter' to Madeline (see page 105) and Madeline wrote a 'bright, charming and amusing note' in reply. Write the two letters, using these prompts to help you.

Eleanor's letter
- happily married to Mr Arabin / new dean of Barchester
- appreciate your friendship / most grateful to you
- forgive Bertie and Charlotte / wish your family well

Madeline's reply
- delighted to hear news / your large, comfortable house
- Bertie enjoying idleness here / father enjoying lower bills
- many handsome young men / several broken hearts

ACTIVITIES: *After Reading*

3 Mrs Proudie probably spoke to her husband about dismissing Mr Slope before the interview on pages 103–104. Complete Mrs Proudie's side of her conversation with the bishop.

Dr Proudie: You really think I should dismiss Mr Slope, my dear?
Mrs Proudie: _____!
Dr Proudie: Well, to be fair, the Signora is extremely attractive—
Mrs Proudie: _____!
Dr Proudie: Yes, yes, of course. One forgets there is a husband somewhere.
Mrs Proudie: _____
Dr Proudie: Disgraceful, as you say, my dear.
Mrs Proudie: _____
Dr Proudie: Interfered, yes, I suppose he did. But perhaps he thought Mr Harding was the right man for—
Mrs Proudie: _____!
Dr Proudie: Well, well, at least Quiverful is the warden now. Did you want me for something, my dear?
Mrs Proudie: _____
Dr Proudie: At once? And what should I say when he comes in?
Mrs Proudie: _____
Dr Proudie: Leave my employment and this house, yes, I think I've got that. What should I say if he asks why, my dear?
Mrs Proudie: _____
Dr Proudie: I expect you will, my dear. I'm sure he will be in no doubt at all about your disapproval.
Mrs Proudie: _____!
Dr Proudie: No, no, of course I do not approve of – of anything. You are absolutely right, my dear, as you always are.
Mrs Proudie: _____

ACTIVITIES: *After Reading*

4 Here are the thoughts of five characters at different points in the story. Which characters are they, and who or what are they thinking about? What has just happened in the story?

1 'This is wonderful news! I couldn't imagine anyone more suitable for my darling girl. She'll make an excellent vicar's wife – unless – good heavens, that's an interesting idea. I must discuss it with the archdeacon.'

2 'Oh dear, I wonder what's happening in there! Perhaps we won't get the post after all, even though it's been promised to us – I just don't trust that man. Freddy and Sarah need new shoes, and there's the new baby on the way, and I can't get any more meat until I pay the last bill . . .'

3 'Arriving together in the same carriage . . . There can't be any doubt about it now. They'll announce their engagement in the next few days, I expect. It's the end of all my hopes – the only woman I've ever loved. And now I must walk around the gardens, and smile and be pleasant to all these people I don't know.'

4 'That awful man's going to cause a lot of trouble, I can see that. All the clergy are furious with him, and poor Father is quite miserable about the changes he seems to want to bring about. He won't be invited here to Plumstead, anyway!'

5 'That woman! A devil in the shape of an unbelievably beautiful female! How did she find out so much? Laughing at me like that, and singing her stupid song, with everybody watching. Well, one good thing's come out of it – I'm cured! I never want to see her again!'

ACTIVITIES: *After Reading*

5 Here is a page from the local newspaper, reporting on recent events in Barchester. Choose one suitable word for each gap.

THE JUPITER   *Thursday 25th September*

THE NEW DEAN

WE ARE SURE that our readers _____ like us to give a warm _____ to **MR FRANCIS ARABIN** of Oxford, _____ will be the dean of Barchester, _____ the sad death of **Dr Trefoil**. _____ Mr Arabin is single at the _____ , we have heard of his recent _____ to a modest and charming young _____ . We hope to hear of their _____ very soon.

Other News

Mr Slope, one of our most _____ and promising young priests, has suddenly _____ to resign his post as bishop's _____ . We will no longer have the _____ of seeing him in Barchester. Sadly, _____ duties require his presence elsewhere.

Mr _____ , new warden of **Hiram's Hospital**, starts _____ there on Monday. His wife and _____ are moving into the warden's comfortable _____ today. **Mrs Quiverful** said, 'I can't _____ it! It's better than my wildest _____ !' We hope they will be very _____ there.

---

6 How much does the title *Barchester Towers* tell you about the story? Do you prefer titles that tell you what to expect? What are the good points and bad points about these titles, for example? Try to think of some alternative titles of your own.

- The Rise and Fall of a Humble Chaplain
- Cathedral Wars
- Power and the Bishop's Wife
- Eleanor

ABOUT THE AUTHOR

Anthony Trollope (1815–1882) was born in London. His father, a lawyer, was facing financial ruin, but managed to send Anthony to top schools at Harrow and later Winchester. His mother, Frances, began to earn quite a good income from her novel-writing, which helped the family finances. In 1834 Anthony became a junior clerk in the Post Office, and in the 1840s he was sent to Ireland, where he lived for some years, eventually returning to London. He had a very successful career in the Post Office, and was responsible for the introduction in Great Britain of the red pillar box for letters.

During his life he published fifty-four novels, as well as magazine articles, plays, lectures, travel books, and short stories. Most of these were written while he had a full-time job. He used to write, at the rate of 1000 words an hour, in the early morning, before going off to his post office duties.

The Warden (1855), the first of six novels in *The Chronicles of Barsetshire*, is set in the imaginary county of Barset (based on the real county of Somerset, with Winchester as the model for Barchester), and the second novel, *Barchester Towers* (1857), showed him at the height of his powers. Trollope said: 'In the writing of *Barchester Towers* I took great delight. The Bishop and Mrs Proudie were very real to me.' Mrs Proudie, he said, was 'a tyrant, a bully, a would-be priestess, a very vulgar woman.'

Barchester Towers is regarded by many people as Trollope's masterpiece, and in 1982 a very successful BBC television film was made of *The Warden* and *Barchester Towers*.

OXFORD BOOKWORMS LIBRARY

*Classics • Crime & Mystery • Factfiles • Fantasy & Horror
Human Interest • Playscripts • Thriller & Adventure
True Stories • World Stories*

The OXFORD BOOKWORMS LIBRARY provides enjoyable reading in English, with a wide range of classic and modern fiction, non-fiction, and plays. It includes original and adapted texts in seven carefully graded language stages, which take learners from beginner to advanced level. An overview is given on the next pages.

All Stage 1 titles are available as audio recordings, as well as over eighty other titles from Starter to Stage 6. All Starters and many titles at Stages 1 to 4 are specially recommended for younger learners. Every Bookworm is illustrated, and Starters and Factfiles have full-colour illustrations.

The OXFORD BOOKWORMS LIBRARY also offers extensive support. Each book contains an introduction to the story, notes about the author, a glossary, and activities. Additional resources include tests and worksheets, and answers for these and for the activities in the books. There is advice on running a class library, using audio recordings, and the many ways of using Oxford Bookworms in reading programmes. Resource materials are available on the website <www.oup.com/bookworms>.

The *Oxford Bookworms Collection* is a series for advanced learners. It consists of volumes of short stories by well-known authors, both classic and modern. Texts are not abridged or adapted in any way, but carefully selected to be accessible to the advanced student.

You can find details and a full list of titles in the *Oxford Bookworms Library Catalogue* and *Oxford English Language Teaching Catalogues*, and on the website <www.oup.com/bookworms>.

THE OXFORD BOOKWORMS LIBRARY
GRADING AND SAMPLE EXTRACTS

STARTER • 250 HEADWORDS
present simple – present continuous – imperative –
can/cannot, must – *going to* (future) – simple gerunds …

Her phone is ringing – but where is it?

Sally gets out of bed and looks in her bag. No phone. She looks under the bed. No phone. Then she looks behind the door. There is her phone. Sally picks up her phone and answers it. ***Sally's Phone***

STAGE 1 • 400 HEADWORDS
… past simple – coordination with *and, but, or* –
subordination with *before, after, when, because, so* …

I knew him in Persia. He was a famous builder and I worked with him there. For a time I was his friend, but not for long. When he came to Paris, I came after him – I wanted to watch him. He was a very clever, very dangerous man. ***The Phantom of the Opera***

STAGE 2 • 700 HEADWORDS
… present perfect – *will* (future) – *(don't) have to, must not, could* –
comparison of adjectives – simple *if* clauses – past continuous –
tag questions – *ask/tell* + infinitive …

While I was writing these words in my diary, I decided what to do. I must try to escape. I shall try to get down the wall outside. The window is high above the ground, but I have to try. I shall take some of the gold with me – if I escape, perhaps it will be helpful later. ***Dracula***

STAGE 3 • 1000 HEADWORDS

... should, may – present perfect continuous – *used to* – past perfect – causative – relative clauses – indirect statements ...

Of course, it was most important that no one should see Colin, Mary, or Dickon entering the secret garden. So Colin gave orders to the gardeners that they must all keep away from that part of the garden in future. **The Secret Garden**

STAGE 4 • 1400 HEADWORDS

... past perfect continuous – passive (simple forms) – *would* conditional clauses – indirect questions – relatives with *where/when* – gerunds after prepositions/phrases ...

I was glad. Now Hyde could not show his face to the world again. If he did, every honest man in London would be proud to report him to the police. **Dr Jekyll and Mr Hyde**

STAGE 5 • 1800 HEADWORDS

... future continuous – future perfect – passive (modals, continuous forms) – *would have* conditional clauses – modals + perfect infinitive ...

If he had spoken Estella's name, I would have hit him. I was so angry with him, and so depressed about my future, that I could not eat the breakfast. Instead I went straight to the old house. **Great Expectations**

STAGE 6 • 2500 HEADWORDS

... passive (infinitives, gerunds) – advanced modal meanings – clauses of concession, condition

When I stepped up to the piano, I was confident. It was as if I knew that the prodigy side of me really did exist. And when I started to play, I was so caught up in how lovely I looked that I didn't worry how I would sound. **The Joy Luck Club**